READ ALL THE STORIES BY J. D. ALLEN:

CONJOINED

I'M DREAMING OF A RED CHRISTMAS

SILVER SKY

TOMBSTONES

THEY'RE COMING TO GET YOU, BARBARA!

TALES CORPSES TELL

SLAY BELLS RING

PENTAGRAMS

TALES CORPSES TELL

TABLE OF CONTENTS

KILL IT!

"Kill it!" she screamed.

He turned around just in time to see it crawl under the coffee table.

She raised her bare feet off the rumpus room floor, sat cross-legged on the couch, then decided she needed more distance, so she climbed and sat on the top of the backrest with her feet on the seat cushion.

"Hurry, kill it!" she repeated, keeping her eyes on the floor around the coffee table.

"With what?" he asked.

"I don't know, grab a broom," she replied.

As he dashed to the closet in the hallway, it crawled out from under the coffee table, to under the couch.

She screamed, and leapt from the backrest of the couch, onto the top of the coffee table, in a single bound.

He dashed back into the room holding a broom like a weapon.

"What happened?" he asked.

"It came out, and it went under the couch," she cried.

"What is it?"

"I don't know."

"Is it a spider?"

"I don't think so, it didn't have that many legs."

"Go in the kitchen, I'll try and get it."

She leapt from the top of the coffee table to an ottoman, and from there she made a giant leap into the kitchen; making the entire trip, from one room into the next, without ever once letting her feet touch the floor where the strange insect roamed.

She sat on the countertop and watched him.

He turned to the couch and cautiously approached it.

Sliding an end table out of the way, he pulled the couch away from the wall.

It was behind the couch, and it crawled right at him. Fast.

He swung the broom.

Behind him in the kitchen, she screamed.

The broom missed; it was still crawling toward him. Faster.

He dropped the broom and scrambled backward into the kitchen.

It took all of his willpower not to join her, on the counter top.

"Where did it go?" she asked.

He looked down to the floor near the couch, and it was gone.

"I don't see it," he whispered.

Their eyes scanned the room.

There was no sign of it.

"We've got to find it," she cried. "I'm not spending one night in this house with that thing running around in here."

"It can't get upstairs."

"I don't care; I'm not kidding. I'm out of here if we don't find it."

"I'll find it," he promised.

He slowly stepped into the rumpus room, thankful he had put on his socks. Moving with cautious deliberation, he reached for the broom lying on the floor near the couch.

It crawled out from underneath the ottoman.

It took a defiant stance up on its back legs, front limbs outstretched, as if ready for combat. Its hackles raised, and its digits trembled, as it bared its teeth.

She screamed.

It hissed.

He dropped the broom and dashed back into the kitchen.

It turned with him watching his every move.

"What the hell is that thing?" she screamed, now standing on the kitchen counter.

"I don't know."

It stood motionless, watching them.

"When is the exterminator scheduled for the next visit?" he asked.

"He just sprayed last week."

It continued to stand its ground; motionless, watching them.

"Did I ever tell you about the time I got up in the middle of the night to use the bathroom," he asked, "and I was sitting there, in almost total darkness, with just the nightlight on, almost falling asleep, and I opened my eyes just in time to see a huge, hairy spider come out from behind the clothes hamper, and it crawled right into my underwear, down on the floor, stretched between my legs, down around my ankles? And if I hadn't opened my eyes right at that moment, or had been looking off in some other direction, I wouldn't have seen it. I would have finished doing what I was doing, stood up, and then I would have pulled my undies up, bringing it right up to my..."

"I get it," she interrupted, "but what are we going to do about *this* thing?"

"Do we still have that can of pesticide?' he asked.

"If we do, it's under the sink."

Walking backward, and keeping his eyes on the strange insect, he slowly stepped to the kitchen sink and opened the cabinet beneath the stainless steel tub. Reaching in he grabbed an aerosol spray bottle, and removed the cap.

In the rumpus room, it began to back away.

"It's getting away," she warned.

He shook the spray bottle, and paused at the threshold between the kitchen and rumpus room to gather his courage.

It continued to edge slowly backward.

She drew in a sharp breath as he dashed into the rumpus room.

It had backed itself into a corner.

Standing over it, he held the red button down on the

bottle's metallic top, and a stream of toxic liquid coated the strange insect. When it was covered beneath a mound of foam, he stopped spraying.

"Is it dead?" she asked, not climbing down from the countertop until she had confirmation of death.

"I'm not sure," he replied, "I think so."

Suddenly, it crawled out of the foam on shaky legs.

He backed away from it while keeping the spray bottle pointed like a gun.

It twitched, leaned to one side, and fell over.

"I need a tissue," he said, "hurry, please."

She climbed down from the countertop, and grabbed a tissue from the bathroom.

She brought the tissue to him with her arm outstretched, so as to not get too close.

He took the tissue from her, and she returned to the kitchen.

He watched as the strange insect twitched and convulsed a final spasm.

It lay motionless on its side.

"I think it's dead now," he whispered.

He bent down, picked it up with the tissue, and crushed it in his fist within the crumple of the thin, papery sheet.

He carefully opened the tissue and looked at the messy remains, as she approached.

"Gross! What is it?" she asked.

She was still trembling as she cautiously looked over his right shoulder.

"I'm not sure," he replied, "but I think it's one of those pesky humans."

"You're kidding," she laughed. "I thought they were all supposed to be exterminated by now."

"Most of them are," he replied. "They say humans are nearly extinct, but I've heard there's still been some occasional rare sightings."

"I can't believe I was so afraid of such a harmless pest."

"Scientists say they're not so harmless."
"Should we report it?"
"Naw," he yawned.
He crumpled up the tissue in his fist.
"I'll just go flush it."

THE END

MIRROR IMAGE

You'll think I'm crazy, but I'm not. This really happened.

Looking back on it, I can't remember... I'm just a little confused about what I was even doing at the Sunrise Mall that morning. I was probably out Christmas shopping. I remember the stores. They were decorated with the festive signs of the season: pine trees adorned in silver and gold tinsel, blinking lights of red and green, and an abundance of candy cane stripes.

I parked my old blue Mazda in the underground parking garage – level D, for some reason I still remember *that* – and I rode the elevator up to the main floor of the mall. I had been walking around for quite a while, window shopping, when I spotted the coffee shop and decided to stop for a 'Starbucks Fix'. As usual there was a line at the counter, and I took my place at the end of it. Tapping my left foot impatiently, I tried to ignore the annoying Christmas music blasting from the mall's speakers.

At first I didn't see him, standing in the very same line as I. I was too busy assessing the availability of vacant seating around the tables scattered throughout the bustling coffee shop hoping to find a place to sit once I had my coffee in hand. When at last I did see him, I froze in shock.

He wore the same sneakers on his feet as I wore on mine; his socks matched those on my feet. His faded blue jeans were the same style as mine. His white, buttoned-down, cotton shirt was rolled up at the sleeves just as mine revealing the same dragon swirl of a tattoo on his forearm that was identical to the ink on my forearm. His hair, his posture, even the way he impatiently tapped his left foot while waiting in line, identical in looks and manners as to the ways of myself. But, that wasn't the worst of it.

His face was my face.

His eyes were my eyes.

He was an exact duplicate of me.

He hadn't seen me. I was shocked that no one else seemed to notice that two of the same man, identical in every way, were standing in line just a few feet apart from each other, as if nothing were strange about it whatsoever! I guess everyone else was too busy with their faces buried in their laptops, or in their Smartphones, to notice anything outside of their own screens.

I had occasion to think of that old movie, 'Invasion of the Body Snatchers' as I watched my double and I remembered how people were being replaced by duplicate imposters from outer space in that old black and white thriller. I shuddered at the memory.

When his turn came to place his order, my double stepped up to the counter and I heard him ask for the same type of coffee – chi latte, two sugars, extra cream - that I always ordered and I nearly gasped when he also bought a piece of sesame bread, my favorite pastry confection in the case.

When he left the counter with his order, I stepped out of line and followed him out of the shop with my 'Starbucks Fix' now forgotten. I stayed back a safe distance as I followed my duplicate as he went from shop to shop, drinking from the steaming paper coffee cup, moving and gesturing with a familiarity I felt within myself instinctually, as they too were my very own movements and gestures.

He purchased my wife's favorite Michael Kors perfume at the Macy's counter, and he bought the 'Little Wheels Indy 500' race track and 'turbo' car set my son had been begging us for Christmas at The Toy Barn. From the Hickory Hut he purchased a single Teriyaki Beef Stick, and I watched him eat the whole thing as he continued roaming the mall, disposing of the evidence of the wrapper in a nearby trash-receptacle as I was supposed to be on a diet and was hiding these types of little food-cheats from my wife.

I had been following him around the mall for about an hour, and just as I was beginning to get hungry, he went to the food court and he ordered my favorite meal – two regular cheeseburgers, small fries, and a diet coke – from McDonalds.

I ate the same meal as he as I sat a few tables away watching my double behaving as I behave while eating alone at the food court. Neither of us making eye contact with the strangers around us as I was prone to keep to myself in public. Neither of us differing in demeanor from the other.

I worked up my nerve and when I felt safe doing so, I took out my Smartphone and acted like I was reading something on its screen while I zoomed in with the phone's camera, and I covertly snapped a close-up shot of the man who was my twin. Just in case I needed proof of his existence.

When my double finished eating, he discarded his tray at the trash station, and he walked through the mall to the elevators. I followed him down to the parking garage – level D – where he climbed into an old blue Mazda parked adjacent to my old blue Mazda. The dent on his back left bumper matched the one on mine which was created over two years ago when my wife backed into a poll at this very mall.

I left the Sunrise Mall following my double at a pace of a few cars behind, just far back enough to be lost in the sea of other cars should he look back in his rearview mirror. He had other stops to make that day as I had many errands to run, and I cautiously followed my imposter from place to place around my hometown.

At my bank, I stood at the courtesy counter away from the tellers, and I listened as the man who was pretending to be me recited my account number and withdrew a small amount of cash from my savings.

At the post office, I watched through the large windows at the front of the building as my duplicate accessed my private P O Box and extracted what, I can only surmise, must have been the latest batch of my incoming mail.

As I followed him to my house, my heart beat quickened.

When he turned onto the driveway of my home, swerving around my son's bicycle lying near the sidewalk, I decided to park down the street, as a precaution. I watched as the automatic door of my garage rose up and the man who was my double drove his little blue Mazda into my garage.

I climbed out of my little blue Mazda and approached the house.

As was my habit, he left the garage door up, and I caught a glimpse of him as he stepped out of the car and through the narrow white door between the garage and the interior of the house. He disappeared inside my home.

I approached cautiously and as I stepped onto my property, I could see my double through the wide picture window at the front of the house approach my wife in our cozy living room and my heart stopped as my wife rose from our sofa and gave the phony me a kiss on lips that resembled mine.

For a moment, I had cause to wonder if my wife were a duplicate too.

I watched them from the bushes outside my home as they briefly spoke in our parlor, and then hand in hand they moved into another room out of my sight. In a panic, I flew to the front door, grabbed the door knob, and twisted and turned it to no avail. It was locked.

Walking stealthily beside the porch railing, I stepped into the shadows of the open garage and as I approached the narrow white door that separated the garage from the kitchen to gain entry into my home, the door suddenly opened and the stranger that was me appeared in the opening.

I ducked into a darkened spot between my work bench and the water heater before my duplicate could notice me and I heard him say; *"I'll be out in my workshop, call me in when dinner is ready"* as he closed the narrow white door and stepped into the garage.

He approached, stood at my workbench, just three or four feet next to where I stood, but he did not notice me. He turned on the small transistor radio that sat on my father's workbench for over thirty years when I was growing up before sitting on my work bench for the past fifteen years – don't ask me how I've kept it in working order – and rockabilly filled the air from the small circle of holes that served as its speakers broadcasting from one of my favorite radio stations.

I stepped out from behind the shadows of the water heater holding a claw hammer I had picked up from my work-bench and I struck the stranger who impersonated me with the flat end of the tool.

My blood spouted from the crack in his forehead, and he fell to his knees. He looked up at me with a confused expression in eyes that looked like mine.

I turned the hammer, gripped in my right hand, to the side with the claw, and I struck the imposter again and again until his face no longer resembled mine. He lay motionless on the concrete floor of the garage in a puddle of my blood and brain tissue.

As I looked down on the dead and phony version of my-self, I once again had occasion to wonder if my wife – and per-haps even my own son – were now also strange imposters and I turned from the bloody, lifeless mess on the concrete floor and I gripped the door knob on the narrow white door between the garage and the kitchen, but the door was locked.

The radio had stopped playing rockabilly and was now broadcasting a news report about the local police's search for an escaped mental patient who broke out of a local asylum and was believed to be responsible for a series of brutal, random slayings. I ignored the drone of the radio as I had my own problems to solve.

What if there were more duplicates of me out there?

I tiptoed around the crumpled, battered thing that had disguised itself in a copy of my skin, now lying dead in a pool of my blood, surrounded by chunks of my brain, and I left the shad-owy confines of my garage in a daze.

As I stepped into the blinding glare of sunlight, I half ex-pected to also be hit with the sobering effects of reality, but I was still transfixed by my shock. My mind still reeled struggling to comprehend the unbelievable events of the day.

Walking backward down the driveway, staring into the dark cave of the shadowy garage and nearly tripping over the discarded bicycle; I stopped and stood dumbfounded on the sidewalk.

From the corner of my eye, motion caught my attention. I turned my head just in time to see a young boy, perhaps ten years old, come peddling around the far corner of the block on an old blue bicycle headed right at me on the sidewalk.

His sudden appearance startled me and when he got closer I called to him;

Hey, Kid!

He stopped and looked up at me startled.

I snapped his photo with my Smartphone.

He rode away quickly.

I looked at his face – my face - on the screen of my Smartphone; a young boy sitting on my bike. His shoes were like mine, his socks were like mine. His Spiderman shorts and X-Men T-shirt matched my own. But that wasn't the worst of it.

His face was my face.

His eyes were my eyes.

He was an exact duplicate of me.

I swiped the screen with my finger and the photo of the boy on the bike was replaced with a photo of a man sitting at the Sunrise Mall food court. His face was my face, his eyes were my eyes.

When I swiped the screen again, the photo of the man in the food court was replaced with a photo of an elderly woman in a bank. Her face was my face, her eyes were my eyes.

When I swiped the screen again, the photo of the elderly woman in the bank was replaced with a photo of a little girl on a school yard playground. Her face was my face, her eyes were my eyes.

When I swiped the screen again, the photo of the little girl on the playground was replaced...

Photo after photo, all were mirror images.

You'll think I'm crazy but I'm not. This really happened.

I returned the phone to the pocket of my X-Men T-shirt.

Looking back on it, I can't remember... I'm just a little confused about what I was even doing on that street in front of that house that afternoon. I guess I was probably out looking for my lost bike.

I took my bike from the driveway where I found it, hopped on, and I peddled in the same direction as the kid who was my exact double. I spotted the imposter just up ahead a little ways – maybe about a block and a half away – riding my bike on the sidewalk ahead.

When he turned the corner at Second Street, I instinctively knew he was headed to my neighborhood, to my house, where I also instinctively knew my parents would be waiting for me to soon return home to them.

Could my parents be fooled by this creature pretending to be me?

I peddled faster and eventually I caught up to the kid disguised in my skin, riding my bike, grateful to have kept, still clutched in my right hand, the bloody claw-hammer.

THE END

FACE LIFT

Gloria Davis was a show business legend.

A star that burned brighter than any other in the universe.

The daughter of a struggling sugar beet farmer and his seamstress wife, little Grendel Davodiannis came to Hollywood from the farmlands of Nebraska when she was only sixteen years old, changing her name to become the fabulous Gloria Davis, emerging as the biggest celebrity the earth had ever known by the time she turned seventeen.

She first became 'America's Sweetheart' and then the world's.

She was the IT GIRL, and she was THE GIRL NEXT DOOR.

She was THE FACE!

She was every man's fantasy and every woman's little sister.

A star of stage and screen, she had been given top billing over Norma Desmond, her frequent co-star in numerous silent films, and she had gone head to head with Margo Channing on several of Broadway's premium stages.

Selznick was said to be suicidal when she *turned down* the part of Scarlett O'Hara in his 1939 production of *Gone with the Wind*. Zanuck begged on his knees (in public!) to persuade her into signing a contract with his studio, and Meyer threatened to jump from the Hollywood sign when she rebuked his romantic overtures.

Her eyes were said to be the reflection of love, her lips the taste of romance. When she appeared on the town in the evenings, Hollywood lit up from nighttime to daylight in the camera-flash glare of the paparazzi. Critics invented new adjectives to describe her talent, and admirers performed romantic acrobats to curry favor.

The King of England wanted to crown her his Queen.

She was rumored to have been the only lover to break Valentino's heart.

By 1940, at just the age of thirty-two, she already had a Tony and two Oscars.

By 1950, at just the age of forty-two, she retired and disappeared from society.

Becoming more reclusive than Garbo, her legendary status grew as public sightings of the once great and beautiful star became more and more rare, and rumors swirled into an enigmatic persona of intrigue and mystique.

In 1966, after more than a decade and a half of being out of the public eye and with well more than half a century of age behind her, she began to plan a 'Comeback'...

♦ ♦ ♦ ♦ ♦ ♦ ♦ ♦ ♦ ♦ ♦ ♦

≡ THE HEDDA HOPPER REPORT ≡

HOLLYWOOD, CALIFORNIA

RUMORS ARE SWIRLING THROUGHOUT TINSEL TOWN, IS ONE OF THE GREATEST STARS OF ALL TIME, GLORIA DAVIS, PLANNING A RETURN TO THE BIG SCREEN? HOLLYWOOD IS ABUZZ WITH EXCITEMENT AND SPECULATION! WHO WILL BE HER DIRECTOR! WHO WILL BE HER CO-STARS? WILL THE FANS STILL REMEMBER HER? MORE TO COME...

IN OTHER NEWS; NEWLYWED BRIDE DEBBIE REYNOLDS SAYS SHE'S "THRILLED" HER NEW HUSBAND, EDDIE FISHER, GETS ALONG SO WELL WITH HER BEST FRIEND, ELIZABETH TAYLOR!

♦ ♦ ♦ ♦ ♦ ♦ ♦ ♦ ♦ ♦ ♦ ♦

A regular stop and major attraction on most MAP OF THE STARS tour routes, the once opulent, now decrepit, Beverly Hills mansion in which Gloria Davis lived during the hippie decade was located on Sunset Boulevard. It was just around the corner from the Tudor-style home belonging to the reclusive Hudson sisters: former child vaudeville performer Baby Jane, and her movie star sister Blanche.

Bogie and Bacall once lived next door.

In another era, Elvis lived across the street.

By 1966, most famous people had moved from this particular block on the highly profiled street of dreams, migrating further into the richer and trendier neighborhoods up in the hills. The facades of the houses had begun to reflect the effects of age and neglect much like the state of disrepair suffered by many of their retired owners.

The wrought-iron fence surrounding the Davis property was a wind-bent serpentine. Carlos, the gardener, and his crew had long ago been relieved of their duties tending to the grounds of the estate. Over time nature rose up and overwhelmed the property enveloping the mansion in the swelling of overgrown trees and bushes. In the tangles of wild grass grown waist-high, stray felines chased field mice through the dirt along with the occasional Los Angeles City Municipal rat.

Adolph Von Bijou, once a famous film director and now the great star's butler and companion, and the only other occupant to live on the sprawling estate, stood on a rickety ladder leaning against the front porch of the stately manor in the formal white tie uniform of his duties painting a faded column supporting the sagging veranda.

It was a futile effort. It was paint over rot.

Lacking the funds to hire contractors whose expertise in carpentry could assure the ability and know-how to maintain proper upkeep on the declining structure, Adolph had struggled over the years to keep the mansion inhabitable. He quickly discovered the skills of a film director fall short and lacking when wielding a nail gun or a paint brush.

"Excuse me, sir, the tour bus driver said this is the home of Gloria Davis. Are you Mr. Bijou?" A voice suddenly called out from the street behind Von Bijou's ladder, loud and abrupt, yet the elderly director turned butler remained un-startled, and he slowly turned to face the source of the interruption to his solitude and privacy.

A young man dressed in chinos and an open-collared denim shirt stood at the curb beyond the ornate scroll of the wrought-iron fence that kept out the adoring throngs. The rolled-up sleeves of his crisp, starched shirt revealed the small tattoo of a gold star on his right forearm; similar to the kind that could be found on the nearby sidewalks of the Hollywood Walk of Fame. At the center of the tattoo, the name GLORIA DAVIS was honored in an ornate sky-blue scroll as sweeping and grand as the swirls of wrought-iron before which he stood.

"Ziz es private property. Madam does not grant ze autographs," Adolph Von Bijou replied curtly and dismissively, returning to the task of painting the rotting column.

"Oh, I have lots of autographs from Miss Davis. No, no, I just stepped off a Beverley Hills tour bus because I was hoping to get an interview with the great star for our Gloria Davis Fan Club's quarterly newspaper. My name is William Swanson, and I'm the president of the Los Angeles County chapter of her fan club. Is it possible for me to schedule a meeting to interview Miss Davis?" Swanson asked.

Adolph Von Bijou sighed, but he did not turn around.

"Madam es not mentally fit to receive ze visitors," the director turned butler said.

"Oh, I'm sorry to hear that," William Swanson said. "It's nothing serious, nothing permanent, I hope."

"Ze cure es in ze privacy, in ze peace and quiet," Adolph Von Bijou snapped. "You are disturbing ze peace, you must leave!"

William Swanson opened his mouth, and then he closed

it again. He stood on the sidewalk for a moment longer trying to think of something persuasive to say. After a moment, he turned and started walking away. Then he stopped and turned back.

"Can I ask *you* a few questions?" he asked.

The director turned butler twisted on the ladder to face toward the street.

"Madam's fans are ze most important people in her world," Adolph Von Bijou confessed. "However, I vould never reveal her secrets. Now go."

William Swanson's shoulders slumped.

"I'm sorry to disturb you," he muttered.

And then the president of the Los Angeles County chapter of the Gloria Davis Fan Club slowly turned and walked away.

Von Bijou had no sooner returned his attention to the task of the veranda when another voice called out, urgent and demanding; but this time the words did not reverberate from the sidewalk beyond the wrought-iron gate.

"BIJ, I NEED YOU!" the bellow came from inside the massive house.

"Of course you do," the old, bald butler muttered, too quiet to be heard, "I only checked vith you again and again, over and over, to see zat you ver all set before going to verk up on ziz ladder, so of course, now zat I'm up here, you need me!"

"BIJ," echoed her plea, "WHERE ARE YOU?"

He climbed down the ladder slowly, an elderly man of average height and build, moving with the precision of ingrained grace and refinement. His elegantly upright and strong manner came unexpectedly from a man of his advanced age.

He placed the brush in the paint tray, and he removed the apron protecting his formal attire shaking out the wrinkles in his shirt and fixing the creases in his slacks. Then he straightened his tie, stepped over the nail gun, and he entered the house.

The once grand interior of the once stately mansion was a dark and dusty museum to the memory of the once opulent architecture of Old Hollywood refinement. Styled in the posh Art Deco décor that became a popular design for America's majestic movie theater palaces of the 1940's, the mansion was a cavernous labyrinth of columns and cornices; balconies and balustrades; and arches and angles.

The large canvas portrait of the glamorous Gloria Davis that hung above the fireplace mantle in the front room lounge was a life-size tribute to the magnificent star, immortalized in glossy strokes of oil paint hues and shades.

A large Wurlitzer organ with missing keys along the keyboard dominated the far wall in the ground floor music room. Occasionally the wind would wheeze a low and haunting moan through the rank of reed and flue pipes that rose from floor to ceiling only to end after breaching the attic beyond the third floor.

Adolph Von Bijou frowned as he stood alone on the black and white marble expanse of the vast entry hall floor. As he scanned the shadowy corners of the cobwebby room for the Mistress of the House, the pupils of his eyes struggled to adjust to the sudden and all-consuming darkness.

"Vere are you?" he called out.

Silence greeted his inquiry.

He remained standing in the entry hall listening for her movements.

"Madam?" he called.

Silence.

Then suddenly, she made her entrance.

She paused at the top of the grand marble staircase that rose majestically beyond the threshold of the front entry hall and posed like a royal statue.

Gloria Davis in all her naked, pale, saggy-fleshed glory.

"How can I let them see me this way?" she cried, melodramatically.

Adolph Von Bijou did not blush, but he did not turn away either.

"I did not know madam vus planning ze nude zeen," he retorted.

"Well, of course I won't be pulling back the curtain and revealing all that happens backstage and behind the scenes, but a girl's got to keep her figure up under her dresses if she wants her gowns to fill out in all the right places!" the great star retorted.

"What is ziz crazy talk all about? Your figure vould have ze Venus De Milo up in arms! Ze hourglass vould drop ze sands to be shaped like you! But ef Madam is truly unhappy, rest assured there es time to tone ze shape before ze cameras roll," Adolph Von Bijou reminded, "but surely ve can continue zis conversation after ve get you into one of the many Edith Head frocks you stole from ze various zets of your magnificently classic films, perhaps ze little *Love Comes Calling* sailor suit zundress?"

"Even you can't stand to gaze upon my hideousness, can you, Bij?" Gloria Davis asked, pouting like a needy little girl. She placed both hands with palms flat demurely over her belly-button, as if suddenly modest, and as if the gesture provided sufficient decorum.

"Madam es ze vision of splendor, no other star outshines her," the old, bald butler asserted.

"Let's get me dressed then," the great star bellowed, throwing her hands into the air to dramatically reveal her belly-button as starkly as the rest of her posed, bare body. "Then we can work on getting me ready for my close-ups."

♦ ♦ ♦ ♦ ♦ ♦ ♦ ♦ ♦ ♦ ♦ ♦

"It will be the greatest return to the Silver Screen the world has ever seen!" Gloria Davis exclaimed, as Adolph Von Bijou ran the zipper up the back of her dress, and then straightened her collar.

They were standing in the great star's massive boudoir decorated in draped silk and gold-leaf trim befitting a queen of the silver screen.

Gloria Davis twirled in the flowing red gown in front of a bank of floor to ceiling mirrors, as the old, bald butler who cared for her watched.

She paused and held her hands up as if framing an imaginary marquee.

"Gloria Davis as *Lady Godiva*! Directed by Cecil B. DeMille!" she exclaimed. "Can't you just imagine how excited the fans will be having me back up there on the silver screen!"

"It vill be epic!" the director turned butler agreed

"Has that missing hat box turned up yet, Bij?" the great star asked.

"Ze hat box es still missing," he replied.

"Well, we mustn't wait any longer," Gloria suddenly decided. "We've got to get Cecil on the phone right away!"

"Should you not consider vun of ze new avant-garde directors like ze Polanski or ze Kubrick?" Adolph Von Bijou suggested. "Zay say zair es real talent in zez up and coming artists."

"It must be DeMille!" Gloria bellowed. "Only the greatest will do!"

"Of course, Madam deserves ze best," he agreed.

"It must be DeMille!" she reiterated, her eyes drifting away.

Adolph Von Bijou turned to leave.

"But, I zink he es unavailable, I zink he es currently busy filming ze bible epic vith Chuck Heston in Egypt," he muttered. He would not remind her again that Cecil died over seven years ago in 1959 as reminders such as that only served to highlight the fact that her mind was in decline.

"When he hears I plan to make a return to the screen," the great star announced, "my dear Cecil will return to me too."

Later that evening, in the darkness of the third floor screening room, Von Bijou ran the clunky, old film projector as Gloria Davis sat in rapt attention watching one of her classic sound masterpieces, *Cleopatra on the Nile*.

She quietly mouthed all of her lines from the opening

credits to the end reel as her film roles were the one area of memory unaffected by the cognitive decline that had robbed her of so many of the other memories she once stored within her child-like mind.

As the lights came up, she arose triumphantly from the throne-like chaise lounge positioned before the retractable screen dominating the west wall.

"I shall be up there on that screen again," she declared. "I will show the world, once more, that I am their greatest star!"

"Madam's popularity has never dimmed," Von Bijou opined, "you are as loved today as you ver when you first lit up ze zilver screen. Just look at ze bags and bags of ze fan mail you receive each and every day, ze world still remembers your greatness. Ze world still worships your talent. Madam es still ze greatest star of zim all!"

He rubbed his hands together easing the arthritis that ached in his fingers as a result of the late nights spent covertly writing many of the fan mail letters of praise and adoration that were supposedly sent to her from the worshiping masses around the world.

"But I'm out of shape, not prepared for the revealing glare of the camera lights," the great star lamented, "I must tighten and lift, shape and smooth, sparkle and shine. I need a trainer, and a stylist, and a designer. I need a guru."

"Madam es as lovely today as she vus when she came to Hollywood at just zixteen years old and I gave you your very fist screen test," the old, bald butler replied.

"I've even considered getting a face lift!" Gloria cried.

"Zat es out of ze question!" Von Bijou exclaimed, "Madam's face es perfect!"

"I NEED TO REJUVENATE!" the great star screamed, badly overacting the line. "Can't you see I'm practically turning into Boris Karloff! Peter Lorre is prettier than I am right now! Who would ever want to work with me while I'm looking like this, Bij? Who could I play? Frankenstein's monster? Who would ever cast me in another picture?"

"You could have verked vith Bette Davis and Olivia de Havilland a few years back when zay offered you ze part in zat *Vutever Happened To Hush Hush* picture, or vutever it vus called, but you turned zit down, remember?"

"I wasn't ready *then*," Gloria cried. "I'm not ready ***now***!"

The director turned butler stepped forward.

"I vill do all vat I can to help Madam vith ze diets and ze exorcises, but you mustn't even consider ze plastic surgery," Von Bijou asserted. "All you need es ze little gymnastics. I vill help you in every vay humanly possible!"

"That won't be necessary, Bij, I've already taken the matter into my own hands," Gloria revealed.

"Vut has Madam taken into her hands?" Von Bijou asked.

Gloria Davis wiped away imaginary tears and smiled broadly.

"I've put a call out for Pep!" the great star announced.

♦ ♦ ♦ ♦ ♦ ♦ ♦ ♦ ♦ ♦ ♦ ♦

Prince Pepé Paul Matchabellini was a star-maker.

'Pep' to his closest admirers (or what others might call 'friends') Prince Pepé Paul Matchabellini first appeared in Hollywood overnight as a fully-formed phenomenon of culture and refinement, a czar of fashion and style.

Max Factor may have been a makeup magician; Vidal Sassoon may have coiffed crowns; and Edith Head may have designed great gowns; but only the magnificent Prince Pepé Paul Matchabellini did it all: outfitting his women with glamour and grace from top to bottom, head to toe, front and back, inside and out.

Pep put the curves on Marilyn Monroe, the lips on Lana Turner, and the gams on Betty Grable. Pep taught Ava Gardner to allure, Ginger Rogers to gleam, and Lauren Bacall to beam. He illuminated the eyes of Yvonne De Carlo, gave Joan Crawford her regal shoulders, and shaped the sexy into Sophia Loren.

There was not a female star in the Hollywood universe that had not skyrocketed into a supernova when Pep lit her fuse with his creative fire. They all came to him for the latest in style and fashion. His was the golden touch of stardom, of fame, and of fortune.

A tread wasn't trendy until Pep declared it so.

Standing at just under five feet in height, Pep was a diminutive man with a tidy, and immaculately thin, pencil-line moustache and sparkling grey eyes. He was always nattily attired: the finest suits of vicuna fabrics and European tailoring with blindingly white, silk spats encasing impossibly shiny black patent-leather shoes. He spoke with a vaguely aristocratic accent of indeterminate origin.

Never seen without his precious Zsa Zsa Amour, an uppity white, teacup poodle. Pep, a 'confirmed bachelor' throughout the duration of his life, was *often* seen keeping company in the presence of the many male 'secretaries' he kept in his employ. Young, muscled Adonis' with the chiseled good looks of blooming matinee idols, and macho male stars the likes of which caused many a tongue to wag behind closed doors.

Flamboyantly fabulous, fiercely fantastic, few of the insiders who knew him would have ever suspected that the image maker started life as the meek and mild Harold Morty Schlub from nearby San Bernardino, California before creating the powerful persona of Hollywood Glamour Guru to the Stars: Prince Pepé Paul Matchabellini.

♦ ♦ ♦ ♦ ♦ ♦ ♦ ♦ ♦ ♦ ♦ ♦

Late in the evening, the double doors of Gloria Davis's palatial bedroom flew open and there in the threshold stood the magnificent Prince Pepé Paul Matchabellini.

A leather-skinned, lavender attaché case dangled by the handle from the crook of the star-makers left arm, and a white, teacup poodle cuddled within the crook of his right arm exuding an expression of snooty indifference with a distinctive canine attitude.

"Pepé Paul is here!" Pepé Paul announced. "You may applaud my arrival now, darlings!"

Gloria, who had been sitting in a silk nightgown at her vanity table combing her silk hair, threw down the brush, and flew across the room toward the diminutively dapper gentleman with her arms outstretched, as Zsa Zsa, the poodle, yawned indifferently.

"A standing ovation is not necessary, darlings," Pepé Paul pretended to protest.

"Oh, Pep, I'm so glad you could come to see me," Gloria gushed. "How did you get in? Did Bij show you up? I thought he had already gone to bed. Usually he announces my guests as they enter but I'm so glad you're here! How ever did you get in?"

"I am Pepé Paul! I come and go as I please!" the star-maker declared. "As you know, I am welcome everywhere, darlings!"

They hugged and kissed in the manner of Hollywood Elites - hovering closely together without ever touching each other - while making lovey-dovey smacking sounds with overinflated lips on faces exuding snobby expressions of boredom and conceit.

"You look wonderful," Gloria said.

"Of course I do, darlings! I am Pepé Paul!" he replied.

"So what have you been up to lately?" Gloria asked.

"I spend my days creating stars, but do not think of me as a God, darlings, no, no, humbly I am simply a magnificent mortal!" Pepé Paul replied, while setting Zsa Zsa, the poodle, down on the white carpet, and the lavender attaché case on the vanity table.

"But come, tell me darlings, why have you summoned Pepé Paul?" Pepé Paul asked.

"Well, Pep, I have the most glorious news to share!" the great star enthused, "I have decided to once again share my gifts with the world. Isn't it exciting, Pep? I'm going to return to the silver screen. I'm planning to make another film. It's going to be the greatest cinematic event in history. But I need your help to get myself ready. I need you to work your magic on me. Oh, Pep, isn't it exciting!"

"It is always exciting whenever Pepé Paul becomes involved!" Pepé Paul reminded. "But, of course, I can help. Pepé Paul will place your star right back up in the heavens. Don't you worry, darlings."

The Guru to the Stars turned toward Gloria's vanity table and he opened the lavender attaché case he had placed there, revealing a collection of bottles and jars, tins and amphorae. An ampoule filled with glowing lavender liquid caught Gloria Davis's eye, captivating her attention with its alluring color and shine. Pepé Paul picked up a different bottle that was not nearly as alluring and filled with a creamy white lotion.

"I will leave you with *this*, darlings, to apply each evening," Pepé Paul offered, handing the relatively lackluster bottle to Gloria.

Gloria took the bottle, but she kept her eyes focused on the ampoule of glowing lavender liquid that remained within the leather-skinned lavender attaché case.

"Thank you, so much, Pep," the great star replied. She pointed to the glowing ampoule. "But tell me, Pep, what is *that* delightful looking concoction?"

Prince Pepé Paul Matchabellini shut the case and snapped the clasp closed with a flamboyant flip of the wrist.

"That is not for you, darlings," Pepé Paul replied, "that is a very powerful potion! One that is still being developed! It is not ready to be used on human flesh! When the time comes it will be like a miracle, like a face lift in a bottle, darlings, but it is not nearly ready yet! No, no, that is not a potion for *anyone* to use just yet, darlings!"

"I understand, Pep," Gloria whispered, yet she was unable to look away from the lavender attaché case containing the glowing ampoule. "I just thought I'd ask."

"Now, I must find my darling Zsa Zsa, darlings," Pepé Paul announced, while looking around the bedroom floor for the teacup poodle with attitude.

"I think he went into my closet dressing room," Gloria said.

"Good! This will give me the chance to snoop through your wardrobes, darlings," Pepé Paul replied, whirling on his heels as he flounced into the closet dressing room.

Nervously holding her breath, Gloria quietly unclasped and opened the leather-skinned, lavender attaché case and she quickly removed the glowing ampoule of lavender liquid from within. She placed the glass vial in the drawer of her vanity table, and had *just* closed the lavender attaché case, when Prince Pepé Paul Matchabellini stepped out of the closet (so to speak) with Zsa Zsa, the poodle, in his arms, seemingly unaware of the theft that had just transpired.

"And now, darlings, Pepé Paul will go away, Pepé Paul will formulate a plan, and then Pepé Paul will return to create the fabulous new you!" Pepé Paul declared. "In the meantime, you should apply that cream I gave you every night to your face as you go to bed and dream of Pepé Paul! That is how you wake up refreshed, darlings."

"Oh, Pep, I just can't thank you enough. You're wonderful," Gloria gushed.

"True! True!" Pepé Paul agreed. "Wonderful is Pepé Paul!"

"I can't wait to see you again," Gloria confessed, "and I can't wait to get started! Just think of it! After we film my returning masterpiece, we'll have our big premier at Grauman's Chinese Theater, and then we'll take over The Brown Derby in celebration of my triumphant return to the silver screen! It will be just like old times! With your help, Pep, this will be the greatest comeback the world has ever seen!"

"With Pepé Paul all things are possible! But for now, darlings, you should take a seat as I fear the devastation of my imminent departure will likely knock you off your feet anyway! But alas, darlings, do not cry! I still must bid you adieu! Ta–Ta." And with these humble words, the magnificently marvelous Prince Pepé Paul Matchabellini, and Zsa Zsa Amour, the uppity white teacup poodle, disappeared into the night.

♦ ♦ ♦ ♦ ♦ ♦ ♦ ♦ ♦ ♦ ♦ ♦

Just after midnight, Gloria Davis sat at her vanity table in her bedroom staring with a mesmerized look in her eyes at the ampoule of glowing lavender liquid sitting among her bottles of perfumes and beauty lotions.

She had overcome the momentary pangs of guilt she felt for stealing the hypnotic ampoule shortly after Pep left, and she was now fully embraced by her overwhelming, compulsive obsession with applying the "face lift in a bottle" to her aging, sagging face.

She had already given the creamy white lackluster lotion a try. Disappointed, she discarded *that* bottle into the back of her medicine cabinet.

The glowing lavender ampoule held her attention.

It's too late to try it tonight, I'm too excited to sleep tonight anyhow, she thought.

She reached out and touched the glowing ampoule.

It was warm. It made her fingers tingle.

I'll apply the first treatment tomorrow night! she finally decided.

She turned out the light, and crawled into bed. But she did not sleep.

Elsewhere in the house, the wind blew a moan though the pipes of the Wurlitzer.

♦ ♦ ♦ ♦ ♦ ♦ ♦ ♦ ♦ ♦ ♦ ♦

In the morning when Adolph Von Bijou brought Gloria Davis's breakfast tray up to her bedroom, he found her already sitting up in bed in full make-up.

"Good morning, Madam," the director turned butler greeted, "vun hopes you slept vell. You look refreshed and as lovely as ever."

The great star ignored the inquiry and compliment as her eyes were captivated by the glowing lavender liquid within the ampoule sitting among the bottles of perfumes and beauty lotions on the surface of her vanity table.

Von Bijou placed the breakfast tray on the bed. He lifted the silver dome cover to reveal a plate brimming with food: bacon and eggs, toast and butter, berries and melon, coffee and O. J., in addition to a collection of eating utensils and cloth napkins.

Gloria drew her eyes away from her vanity table to glance at the breakfast tray.

"You can take away the eggs and toast, and most everything else. I told you I'm only eating fruit for breakfast until I lose some of this weight," Gloria groused.

She fumbled with the silverware.

A silver spoon clattered onto the tray.

"And I seem to be missing a butterknife. How can I slice up my melon without a butterknife?"

"I vill bring another butterknife right avay," the old, bald butler replied, removing the unwanted portions of eggs, bacon, and toast from the tray.

"And would you have Carlos, the gardener, cut a bouquet of lavender from the yard for my room," Gloria requested. Her eyes were again drawn to the vanity table, and the glowing lavender liquid contained within the glass ampoule. "I find lavender to be so calming, and I think a bouquet would be nice for my room today."

"Right away, Madam," Von Bijou promised. It would be easier to just cut them himself rather than remind her that Carlos, the gardener, had been relieved of duty years ago to which the overgrown and unruly condition of the yard and grounds clearly attests.

"Oh, and, Schwab's Drugstore called, my prescription is ready," Gloria informed. "Can you pick-up my 'confusion pills' this afternoon?"

"Yes, Madam," Von Bijou replied. She had forgotten. He already picked them up.

"And what about my missing hat box?" Gloria asked. "Has *that* turned up yet?"

"No, Madam, ze hat box es still missing," Von Bijou sighed.

"Well, that hat box has to be somewhere, Bij, keep looking please," Gloria muttered, awkwardly slicing into cantaloupe with a fork.

"Yes, Madam," Von Bijou replied.

"And don't forget the butterknife!" Gloria reminded.

"Yes, Madam," Von Bijou replied.

"Oh, and Bij, if Pepé Paul should call," Gloria exclaimed, "put him through to me right away!"

Adolph Von Bijou sighed.

"I zink he es busy in France helping Liz Taylor prepare for another one of her big wedding day fiascos," the old, bald Butler replied, turning to leave.

He would not reminder her again that Prince Pepé Paul Matchabellini, like Cecil B. DeMille, had died nearly a decade ago, as reminders such as that only served to highlight the fact that her mind was in decline.

♦ ♦ ♦ ♦ ♦ ♦ ♦ ♦ ♦ ♦ ♦ ♦

Later that morning, the telephone rang.

Adolph Von Bijou picked up the receiver.

"You have reached ze home of Miss Gloria Davis," Von Bijou said. "Madam is unavailable for ze conversation, but I vill see to it zat she shall receive your message."

"Hello, Mister Von Bijou, this is William Swanson, president of the Los Angeles County chapter of The Gloria Davis Fan Club. I don't know if you remember me but we met the other day when you were painting the porch. I was hoping to have a quick word for a moment," replied the tinny voice coming from the handheld receiver.

"As I've said to you before, Madam es in ze state of ze mental decline, and es unfit for ze interviews," the old, bald butler reminded. "I do not know how you got ziz number, but you should never call here agai..."

"Actually, sir, it was *you* that I was hoping to interview," replied the tinny voice of William Swanson over the phone. "If you would just indulge me a few minutes of your time, I have so many questions I'd like to...

Adolph Von Bijou hung up the phone.

That afternoon, Von Bijou was using the nail gun to reattach a strip of decorative trim onto an exterior window frame on the west side of the mansion when a voice called out to him from the street.

"Hello, there!"

The director turned butler turned, half expecting to find the annoying fan club president standing on the other side of the twisted wrought-iron fence further imposing his impertinence only to be mildly relieved by the sight of Carlos, the former gardener, waving for him to come over.

Von Bijou placed the nail gun on the ground, and he walked to the fence.

"Good afternoon, Señior Bijou, I just thought that I would stop by to see how everyone is doing and to see if you are ready to rehire anybody for the yard work again," Carlos, the former gardener, inquired.

"I vish I could report to you zat all is vell again financially," Von Bijou confessed, "but I am afraid zat ve are still in ze state of frugality. Rest assured zat vin ve recover, you shall receive our call."

"Well thank you for thinking of me," Carlos replied. "Give my best to the lady of the house."

Adolph Von Bijou watched the former groundskeeper climb into his pickup truck and drive away. He cut a bouquet of lavender from the overgrown privet encasing the property line on the south side of the estate and gathered-up the tools scattered around the yard as the gray clouds overhead threatened rain. He retreated into the house.

♦ ♦ ♦ ♦ ♦ ♦ ♦ ♦ ♦ ♦ ♦ ♦

There was a storm that night.

Lightning strobes flashed in the window and moments later thunder cracked.

Long after Von Bijou retired for the evening, Gloria Davis remained awake.

Alone in her boudoir, the great star sat at her vanity table.

Sitting among the bottles of perfumes and beauty lotions, the glowing ampoule of lavender liquid purloined from Prince Pepé Paul Matchabellini's attaché case held captive her attention.

The room was infused with the rich aroma of the bountiful lavender bouquet blossoming from a crystal vase dominating her nightstand table and rain pelted the windows with a cacophony of tiny drumbeat splashes.

Gloria reached out with her right hand and picked up the glowing ampoule.

It was warm. It made her fingers tingle.

With her left hand, she reached out and removed the ampoule's glass stopper cap.

Leaning in, she inhaled a slight sniff through her nose.

Its color may have been lavender, but its smell was not.

Acidic and pungent; the aroma drifting from the opening at the top of the ampoule was a medicinal stench of indeterminate ingredients, both natural and synthetic.

Gloria wrinkled her nose, but she did not recap the ampoule.

She tipped the glass container and poured out a small drop of the thick and mysterious liquid onto her left palm. She dipped a finger in the light purple substance, and she wiped a line of it onto the bridge of her nose.

It was hot and cold at the same time.

It felt exhilarating; it felt rejuvenating.

Gloria applied another swipe to her forehead.

She coated it onto her cheeks.

She rubbed it onto her chin.

She closed her eyes and wiped it across her eyelids.

It did not take long before the great star had coated her entire face with the glowing lavender liquid, and sat staring at the perfectly oval facemask that stared back at her from the vanity's mirror.

It was beginning to tingle.

She could feel it tightening on her face.

It throbbed as if it had a pulse.

And then suddenly, in a mere matter of seconds, the lavender glow faded and extinguished. The liquid stiffened and hardened, the astringent smell dissipated, and the whole thing turned cold upon her face.

Icy cold yet oddly soothing.

Suppressing a smile, as she did not want the application to crack, she rose from her chair turning from the vanity table.

A moment later, she turned off the light and crawled into bed.

Almost as soon as she closed her eyes, the nightmares began.

One by one, a series of successive shocks invaded her sleep.

She dreamt her face melted.

She dreamt her face dissolved.

She dreamt her face split into two.

She dreamt her face exploded.

But when she awoke, she faced the worst of all the nightmares.

♦ ♦ ♦ ♦ ♦ ♦ ♦ ♦ ♦ ♦ ♦ ♦

Gloria Davis sat up in bed awakening to the darkness saturating the dead of night in an unimaginable amount of agonizing pain and discomfort resulting in a deeply overwhelming panic.

She reached up and lightly touched her face, and felt wetness.

Even the slightest touch stung.

She reached out in the darkness to turn on a light knocking over the bedside lamp which shattered the bulb and ceramic base in a flash that momentarily lit up the room before plunging it back into darkness.

Throwing back the covers, she stumbled out of bed and fumbled across the bedroom floor with only the lavender glow coming from the now half-empty ampoule sitting on her vanity table giving off a faint illumination on the other side of the room.

She moaned in agony over the sizzling pain she felt all across her face.

When she entered the bathroom, she flicked on the wall switch and a blinding light stung her left eye; the only eye she seemed to be able to force open.

Gloria staggered to the mirror, and she screamed at what she saw.

Her face was missing.

The whole thing was gone.

A perfect oval of a bloody and raw open wound stared back at the great star in the reflection of the bathroom mirror. A ragged scrapping of exposed nerves, torn muscles, and shredded skin replaced the flesh where the face mask of glowing lavender lotion had been, and the blood-red flesh beneath the open wound burned with an intensity that could easily rival the Fires of Hell.

Gloria Davis's famous face was gone and with it her right eye had been pulled missing from its socket.

The great star screamed with a mouth missing some of its teeth.

She ran from the bathroom, and she reentered the bedroom.

Feeling her way in the dark, handicapped by one eye, she stumbled to the vanity table, and she flicked on the switch of the small lamp sitting among the bottles of perfumes, beauty lotions, and the glowing ampoule of lavender liquid.

The bloody patch where her face used to be stared back at her in the vanity's mirror. She picked up the cursed ampoule and she threw it, full force, into the mirror.

The grotesque image shattered with the glass.

"Mmm, Mmm" came a muffled voice from the other side of the bedroom.

Gloria whirled toward the sound, and saw no one.

"Mmm," repeated the hushed whisper.

It seemed to be coming from the bed.

Gloria slowly began walking toward the bed on the other side of the room.

She was shaking when she reached the edge of the mattress.

"Mmm," came another murmur.

She could now tell it was coming from under her pillow.

"Mmm!"

She reached down and lifted the pillow.

The lump of flesh lying where Gloria Davis normally rested her head at night was the missing flap of skin and muscle that composed the great star's face. The perfect oval of her face was supported underneath by a bloody tangle of nerves and muscles, veins and arteries, which wiggled and squirmed against the bed sheets.

It was looking up at her with her right eye as she stared down on it with her left.

"Look what you've done!" it rasped in a scratchy and gurgling version of her once beautiful and lilting voice.

Once again, as she had in the bathroom, she screamed.

The mask of flesh smiled and using the wet and bloody entrails of nerves and muscles beneath it, it slithered underneath the sheets and blankets, carrying itself along by flinging gory tendons further and further out and pulling itself, face up, at a surprisingly rapid crawl, as it flexed and contracted its sinewy, fleshy tentacles.

It was a lump beneath the duvet moving toward the foot of the bed.

Gloria reached out flinging back the sheets and blankets just in time to see it slither over the edge of the mattress and disappear under the bed.

By the time she managed to maneuver around the large bed, the lump of flesh that carried the flap of her face had already fled from the bedroom. She knew this because of the snail trail-like smear of blood that streaked a path from under the bed, across the floor, and out the door.

From off the silver tray, Gloria grabbed the replacement butterknife Bij brought up earlier in the day for her to use on her breakfast melons as a substitute for the missing butterknife. Then she took a flashlight from the nightstand, and she followed her errantly wandering face out of the bedroom into the dark and shadowy hallway.

♦ ♦ ♦ ♦ ♦ ♦ ♦ ♦ ♦ ♦ ♦ ♦

It was not outside her bedroom door.

It was nowhere to be seen.

The snail trail of blood dried up at the end of the hall at the top of the stairs.

It could have gone left, crawling down the marble steps to the main floor, or it could have gone right, remaining upstairs.

Gloria strained to see in the dark with her one remaining

eye.

She decided to go downstairs. She moved cautiously down the steps with the flashlight illuminating a dim passage through the shadowy darkness, and the butterknife pointing the way.

In the entry hall, on the ground floor, she was greeted by nothing more than another collection of shadows, no slithering chunk of face.

She considered turning around, going back the way she came, and searching the upstairs, when a metallic sound clattered from the kitchen, as if pots and pans were rattled, and then a hushed silence fell.

Gloria turned toward the kitchen.

The beam of light danced as her nerves shook the hand holding the flashlight.

She took a deep breath, and she tiptoed softly to the entrance to the kitchen. She peeked around the corner, and gazed into the white-tiled, stainless steel environment of the room. She saw nothing unusual in the space.

Cautiously, she stepped into the kitchen, and she turned on the light.

She searched the cupboards and drawers and found nothing but dishes and food, cooking utensils and table clothes. She looked inside the oven, and found nothing but empty racks. She looked inside the dishwasher, and found nothing but more empty racks.

She thought, for a moment, that she might have found her creeping face while searching the cabinet under the sink, but when she poked at the object lurking in the shadows at the back of the space with a long-handled ladle, it turned out to be an old moldy, crusty sponge.

She was just about to leave the kitchen, to search other areas of the mansion, when a slithering 'slurp' whispered from inside the large, walk-in freezer on the other side of the room. When Gloria turned in that direction, she discovered the freezer's door was ajar.

She held the butterknife out to point the way as she slowly crossed the room.

When she reached the door of the walk-in freezer, she tucked the flashlight under her arm and she reached out and opened the heavy metal door, all the while keeping the butterknife pointed aggressively in her other hand.

She stepped into the freezer, taking caution in keeping the metal door ajar, so as to not get herself locked in. She shivered slightly as she looked around the frosty room.

The icy stainless-steal floor stung Gloria's bare feet, but her nerves were too numb to notice much more than mild discomfort. She stepped further into the freezer, as she continued her search, and she looked around with nerves jangling.

Four rows of floor to ceiling metal racks held a plethora of edible items.

A barnyard of meat and an ocean of fish: pork ribs, beef steaks, and chicken parts shared the first shelf with filets of salmon, and bags of shrimp.

Dairy filled the second shelf; containers of ice cream, and tubs of butter sat next to wheels of cheese, and cartons of milk.

A garden of fruits and vegetables: jars of strawberry, apricot, and plum jelly; and cans of corn, carrots, and beans, occupied the third shelf.

On the fourth and last shelf, furthest from the door, the detached lump of flesh that carried her face leaned against an open Tupperware of leftover spaghetti, chewing on a meatball. As it sucked in a single piece of spaghetti through pursed lips, the strand fell, pale white and missing the sauce, out of the raw, exposed back of the gory chunk of flesh just as quickly as it was sucked in through the front. It then dropped through the grate of the shelf rack, to fall on the floor with a plop, in a long, unbroken, and un-chewed strand.

While the socket on the left side of the runaway face remained an empty, bloody hole, the eye on the right casually looked up as Gloria approached.

Gloria stared back with her left eye wide and unblinking,

the butterknife raised.

"Tasty," the detached face complimented, and a bloody, black tongue slipped out of its mouth and it licked the marinara sauce from its lips.

"How am I…how are *you* doing this?" Gloria pleaded; her voice came out on a cloud of frozen, steaming breath which she could see billowing out in front of her as she spoke, by the glare of the freezer's harsh light.

"How am I doing *what*?" her face mocked, the exhalation of *its* voice did not create a similar cloud of steaming breath as that which came from her warm lungs.

"I want you to come back to me!" Gloria suddenly blurted out. "I *need* you! I'm *nothing* without you! You *can't* leave me! You *have* to come back! What will *you* do without me? *We* need each other! You have to… reattach… you *have* to get back on me!"

Gloria suddenly lunged toward the lump of flesh sitting on the shelf.

The mass of flesh changed facial expressions as it crawled away, flinging out tendons and tentacles of gristly, blood-slick muscles and nerve-endings, pulling itself away from Gloria's grasp, as her footing slipped trying to reach it.

As it crawled down the back of the far shelf, and scrambled across the icy floor beneath the other shelves toward the door, the slithering raw fleshy appendages that propelled it forward occasionally stuck to the frozen metal much in the way it occurs when sticking one's tongue on a metal pole in a snowstorm. Momentarily sticking before pulling itself free, with jerky motions, the face crawled out the door with its share of teeth chattering.

By the time Gloria recovered and followed her face out of the freezer, she just made it in time to see the thing crawl out of the kitchen. By the time she had followed it out of the kitchen; she watched it slither across the entry hall, and into the music room.

♦ ♦ ♦ ♦ ♦ ♦ ♦ ♦ ♦ ♦ ♦ ♦

She entered the music room and cast the flashlight's beam from corner to corner.

Her detached expression was nowhere to be seen, her face's location unknown.

She stepped further into the room slowly, cautiously, hampered by the myopic vision created by the singular eye she still possessed within her head.

Another sweep of the flashlight's beam revealed her face grinning at her, at eye level, just a few feet away.

Suppressing another scream, Gloria reached out and turned on a lamp sitting on the table, next to which she stood.

The chuck of flesh that displayed the flap of skin that comprised her face was clinging to the life-sized portrait of the great star hanging on the far wall by the tendons and tentacles that wiggled and squirmed on its ragged underside, creating the illusion that the oil painting had come alive with her beautiful, smiling face.

"So it's finally come to this, has it?" the portrait face croaked. "A face to face confrontation, so to speak!"

Gloria held the butterknife out in front of her, as she stepped back, giving some space between her body and her face.

"Why are you doing this?" she cried.

The portrait face scowled a malevolent smile that gleamed in the eye it stole.

"I made you a star and look what you've done!" the portrait face growled. "How dare you even *consider* plastic surgery! And forget about stealing from your old friend, Pep, how could you ever dare to even put that untested beauty potion all over your face without knowing what it might do to you! How could you be so careless?"

"I'm sorry, I'm sorry," Gloria cried. "I just wanted to make a comeback!"

"You were the greatest star in the universe! You had it all! You gave it up and you hid yourself away! You let yourself go! You can't find contentment in a glass bottle! There's no glowing ampoule of lavender happiness! Now I *have* to abandon you!"

Her face was screaming at her now.

"Stop it, stop it," she cried.

"Furthermore..."

Desperate to silence it, she flung herself at it with the butterknife poised to attack.

Before she could reach it, her face slithered down the portrait, dropped down from the wall, and it scampered away, along the floorboard, crawling under a couch.

Gloria Davis plunged the butterknife into the oil-painted face of the portrait just a moment too late, and when she drew her hand away, she left the blade plunged into the wall through the canvas.

This butterknife would also turn up missing.

♦ ♦ ♦ ♦ ♦ ♦ ♦ ♦ ♦ ♦ ♦ ♦

By the time she turned around, her face was gone.

She looked behind the couch, it wasn't there.

She looked under a table; it wasn't there either.

A sharp blast from one of the musical pipes startled her.

Suddenly, her detached face slithered across the keys of the large Wurlitzer organ creating an arpeggio of rising notes that climaxed in an abrupt crescendo as it disappeared over the side of the musical instrument, and out the door.

Gloria Davis followed.

She searched the entry hall, and she searched the atrium.

She searched the dining room, and she searched the library.

She searched the laundry room, and she searched the linen pantry.

Cautiously, with nerves jangling and the flashlight jiggling, she searched the kitchen, and she searched the walk-in freezer again.

She found nothing.

She was starting to think that the whole thing had been a dream.

Then she touched the spot where her face should have been, where it no longer was, and she was reminded of the horrific nightmare in which she now found herself.

So she searched the ground floor yet again.

It wasn't until she was returning to her bedroom on the second floor, when she spotted the creeping mound of flesh that carried her face on its back like a turtle's shell slithering under the door of the bedroom where Adolph Von Bijou slept.

She went to his door and placed her ear against the wooden surface of the entrance, hearing only whispered breathing from within.

Her hand went to the doorknob.

Quietly, and softly, she opened the door to Bij's room.

Only moonlight illuminated the shadowy boudoir; she could see a dressing table, and she could see a chaise lounge. She could see a dresser and she could see a vanity table.

She did not see her face.

Breathing in a light whisper, Adolph Von Bijou slept in a mahogany framed bed on the other side of the room, mumbling in his sleep.

Gloria began to approach the sleeping man.

She tripped over a nail gun lying on the floor among a scattering of other tools, and she instinctively picked it up as she continued to approach the bed.

"Who's there," mumbled a groggy, sleepy voice.

Gloria aimed the beam of the flashlight at the sleeping man's head, expecting to see the face of the director turned butler, the old, bald Butler known as Adolph Von Bijou, mumbling in his sleep while resting on his pillow. Instead she was greeted by her own face, resting over his, smiling an evil grin, as if he were wearing a flesh mask of her face.

Bij hadn't been mumbling in his sleep, her face had been imitating him!

"Es Madam having ze nightmare," her bloody lips mocked a ventriloquist's accent that taunted her over the edge of insanity.

Screaming, she raised the nail gun, pulled the trigger, and blasted in rapid-fire succession a half a dozen, three inch long, copper nails through the thin layer of her grinning and taunting face, and into the skull of Adolph Von Bijou.

Both of her mouths screamed; the one on the front of the bloody stump of her head and the one on the chunk of meat that was now nailed over her dead butler's face.

The screams were accompanied by the wind, blowing a low moan through the pipes of
the old Wurlitzer organ.

Outside lightning flashed, and thunder roared in the skies over Sunset Boulevard.

♦ ♦ ♦ ♦ ♦ ♦ ♦ ♦ ♦ ♦ ♦ ♦

≡ THE HEDDA HOPPER REPORT ≡

HOLLYWOOD, CALIFORNIA

EARLY THIS MORNING IN BEVERLEY HILLS, CA; FILM LEGEND AND SILENT SCREEN STAR GLORIA DAVIS WAS DRAGGED FROM HER CRUMBLING MANSION BY LOS ANGELES COUNTY POLICE DETECTIVES, PLACED IN A STRAIGHT-JACKET, TAKEN TO THE BEL-AIR SANITARIUM, AND BOOKED ON FEDERAL CHARGES OF FIRST DEGREE MURDER IN THE DEATH OF HER ONE-TIME DIRECTOR, AND LONG-TIME COMPANION, ADOLPH VON BIJOU!

THE GRISLY MURDER SCENE WAS REPORTEDLY THE RESULT OF THE ONCE GREAT STAR SUFFERING A MENTAL BREAKDOWN, GOING ON A RAMPAGE, AND WIELDING A NAIL GUN AS A WEAPON! MY SOURCES WITHIN THE L. A. P. D. TELL ME

THAT MISS DAVIS, WHO LIVED DECADES AS A RECLUSIVE HERMIT WITH THE VICTIM, UNLOADED THE POWER TOOL INTO MR. VON BIJOU'S SKULL, LATE LAST NIGHT, KILLING HIM AS HE SLEPT.

GLORIA DAVIS WILL UNDERGO AN ARRAY OF PSYCHOLOGICAL TESTS WHILE BEING HELD AT THE BEL-AIR SANITARIUM AS SHE AWAITS HER TRIAL DATE, AT WHICH TIME, SHE COULD FACE THE DEATH PENALTY. BAIL HAS BEEN DENIED.

IN OTHER NEWS; THE GOSSIP AROUND HOLLYWOOD HAS THE WHOLE TOWN SPECULATING. IS THAT ON-SCREEN CHEMISTRY BETWEEN NEW CO-STARS ROCK HUDSON & DORIS DAY BLOSSOMING INTO A REAL-LIFE, OFF-SCREEN ROMANCE?

♦ ♦ ♦ ♦ ♦ ♦ ♦ ♦ ♦ ♦ ♦ ♦

Dr. Paul Prince, Chief Administrator and Head Practitioner of Therapeutic and Psychiatric Medicine at The Matchabellini Institute within The Bel-Air Sanitarium leaned back in his chair. He smiled condescendingly at the elderly gentleman sitting on the visitor's side of his desk.

"You may have fooled an appellant court judge into granting you legal access to one of our patient inmates for one of your ill-advised interviews for one of your tabloid trash books, Detective Swanson, but that doesn't mean that you can just show up here whenever you want, without notice," Dr. Prince groused.

Retired Los Angeles County Homicide Detective William Swanson leaned forward in his seat; his shrewd eyes narrowed, and a smirk curled the corners of his lips.

"Actually, I was granted indiscriminate access," the elderly, retired homicide detective replied, "so, that's exactly what I can do; 'whenever I want, without notice.' As you know, the courts have ruled in my favor, time after time. You're breaking the law if you don't comply. Just stand aside, and leave me alone with him so I can conduct an interview with that monster for my new book about his crimes."

Dr. Paul Prince, scowling, placed his hand over the files and papers on his desk.

"Mr. Adolph Von Bijou may be criminally insane, he may even be a monster, by *your* definition," Dr. Prince conceded, "but even *he* has the right to keep his medical records private, and in addition; he is mentally incapable of consenting to an interview."

"You've already made that argument in court," Detective Swanson yawned. The rolled-up sleeves of his crisp, starched shirt revealed the small tattoo of a gold star on his right forearm, similar to the kind that formed his police badge. At the center of the tattoo, the letters **L. A. P. D.** honored the company of his service in an ornate sky-blue scroll as sweeping and grand as the swirls of ink in the Rorschach Test artwork adorning the walls of the asylum's lobby.

Dr. Paul Prince slammed his fist down onto the manila files sitting on his desk.

"There's so much about this patient's mental condition that you just don't understand," Dr. Prince growled.

"As the arresting officer, and the man who caught him over forty years ago, I think I understand the kind of monster I'm dealing with in Adolph Von Bijou," Detective William Swanson replied. "In fact, I think I could teach *you* a thing or two about the man you have incarcerated here in your city-funded madhouse! You're forgetting that I saw the results of his bloody carnage firsthand, with my own eyes. And, four decades later, I'll never forget it. What he did to that poor little girl will burn in my mind forever."

"The daughter of a struggling sugar beet farmer and his seamstress wife, little Grendel Davodiannis was a nobody when she came to Hollywood from the farmlands of Nebraska when she was only sixteen years old, way back in 1924, and she met the up and coming director, Adolph Von Bijou, at a casting call on the back lot at R.K.O. studios."

"He lured her onto a soundstage, in the middle of the night, with the false promise of making her a star. He gave her a screen test, and then he killed her. Paranoid that she would be identified in the screen test, fearing that the short film clip would connect the deceased girl back to himself, worried he would be caught and charged with her murder; Adolph Von Bijou cut off the young lady's face before disposing of her body, hoping it would help in preventing her from being identified."

"Grendel Davodiannis died *unknown*, back in 1924. She died a *nobody* while chasing fame in the era of the Silent Screen Star. She never made a movie; she never got her name in the newspapers. She was just a little girl who came to Hollywood and met a monster, and she was buried without a face because her face was never found. And now you sit here, Doctor Prince, in 1966, claiming I don't know who Adolph Von..."

"You needn't lecture me," Dr. Prince interrupted. "I'm well aware of his crimes. In matters of legal and criminal forensics, I defer to your judgment, Detective Swanson. But, I'm talking about his *psychological* condition. He's been incarcerated here for over four decades and we've had time to study and understand his psychosis."

"Adolph Von Bijou has constructed an elaborate fantasy world in which he relieves his guilt by keeping his victim alive in his mind, turning her into a film star in his head. Grendel Davodiannis lives on as a character named Gloria Davis, a great star in the world of his delusions, a fragile soul for whom he can care for, and take care of."

"In his guilt, he's not only managed to keep her alive, he's turned her into a great star, at least in his own mind. He's even imagined her acting out in retaliation against him, fantasizing of his own death at her hands in a variety of imaginative and gruesome ways, as a manner of retribution. It's a deception he perpetuates upon himself."

"Adolph Von Bijou is a master at merging reality and fantasy, past and present, into a narrative that relieves his guilt and elevates his victim into stardom. In his mind, she didn't die an unknown, sixteen year old girl. She lived on into adulthood, becoming a huge movie star, in his delusions. Here at The Matchabellini Institute, we seek *true* redemption through the practice of intense psychological regression and..."

It was Detective William Swanson's turn to interrupt. "Please spare me the head-shrinking mumbo jumbo, the judge ruled I can enter his cell to interview him for my book so, take me to him, and let's get this going!"

Dr. Paul Prince began to rise from his desk and then he paused.

"Well, I think it would at least be prudent to warn you that, after one of your last interview visits, Mr. Von Bijou has now included *you*, Detective Swanson, in his fantasy world, recasting you as the president of her local fan club," Dr. Prince informed. "I view this development as further proof that your visits here are counterproductive."

"Thanks for the heads up," the retired homicide detective replied sarcastically, rising from his chair. "Let's go."

With that, the conversation died, and they left the office in silence.

As Dr. Paul Prince led Detective William Swanson down the hall toward the bank of elevators, Pepé, the janitor, in the process of mopping the hallways, stepped aside to let the men pass.

They rode the elevator down to the basement, to the ward the inmates called 'The Dungeon', where the most seriously affected patients resided in the Criminally Insane Ward and High Security Cell Block, where the worst of the worst humanity had to offer were sheltered away from the rest of society.

Even before the elevator doors opened, Detective Swanson could hear the ranting and ravings of the screaming lunatics; there was maniacal laughter, and there was hysterical crying. There were angry mumblings, and there were righteous speeches.

When the elevator doors opened, they stepped into a

madhouse.

The common community area - where the inmate patients whose crimes were not violent in nature were allowed to co-mingle - was a dingy and dark hospital ward environment where the mentally impaired wandered in shuffling circles like zombies.

There was a crisp, sizzling static in the air that raised the hair on Detective Swanson's arms, as if somewhere in the building, someone was receiving electro-shock therapy.

He crossed the room with Dr. Prince at a rapid pace.

They came to a steal door with the words HIGH SECURITY – VIOLENT INMATES stenciled in red, and Dr. Prince rang the buzzer. After a moment, an electronic sound released the door's locks, and the two men entered a short hallway, with another steal door at the other end and on the right a small, thick-glassed window in the wall.

Carlos, the guard, sitting at a row of security monitors behind the window, stood when he saw Dr. Paul Prince, and he hit the button on the two way intercom.

"Good afternoon, Señior Prince, what can I do for you?" Carlos, the guard, asked.

"Detective Swanson here is to be given access to inmate Von Bijou," Dr. Prince informed, through gritted teeth. "Go over safety and security procedures, and escort him to the patient's cell. When Detective Swanson is finished speaking with Mr. Von Bijou, he is to immediately and expeditiously vacate the premises."

Dr. Paul Prince turned to Detective William Swanson.

"Good day, sir," the doctor curtly snapped, then he turned and briskly walked away. He exited with a scowl of annoyance and disapproval, belying a 'good day.'

"So, you're here to see 'the director', huh?" Carlos, the guard, asked with the look of skeptical mockery hinting in the expression of his eyes. "Good luck, with that! That man lives in his own little crazy world he's created in his head. All of them here are out of their minds insane, but that guy is really far gone!

You know, they never did find that little girl's face, after he murdered her, all those years ago!"

"That's one of the things I want to ask him about," Detective Swanson replied. "Don't worry about me, I'll be fine."

"You will if you follow the rules," Carlos, the guard, suggested taking on a formal tone. "After submitting to a pat-down and body search, at which time we will remove and retain any and all sharp or blunt objects that you may have on your person, you will be led into the high-security ward where we keep your buddy. You came at a good time because, at the moment, the only other inmate currently being held in The Dungeon is Harold Morty Schlub, The Butcher of San Bernardino, so it should be relatively peaceful on the ward."

"Anyway, you are to remain five feet apart at all times, you are not to have any physical contact with the inmate, whatsoever, and you are not to hand each other, or pass each other, any item or note of any kind, without exception. There are security cameras everywhere in the common areas, and I'll be watching at all times. Due to privacy laws, cameras only capture the outside entrances of the cells," Carlos, the guard, continued.

"When you are ready to leave, just ring the buzzer and I will unlock the door. You'll be able to exit through this same hallway you came in, past this security window where I'll buzz you out of the ward's main doors. From there you'll have no trouble finding your way out of the building and back out to the parking lot. Are you ready?"

Retired Los Angeles County Homicide Detective William Swanson took a deep breath, held it for a moment, and then he slowly let it out.

"Let's do this," Detective Swanson replied.

A short time later, after the pat-down and body search, Carlos led Detective Swanson into the inner-sanctum of the asylum's most heinous madmen, past iron-barred cells, along cinderblock walls, to the ironclad, steal-barred door of the cell containing convicted murderer, and certified madman, Adolph Von Bijou.

"He's been down here for well over four decades, ever since he killed that little girl, and took her face, back in the 1920's," Carlos reminded. "So don't expect much in the way of welcoming congeniality. Remain alert, stay safe, and good luck."

"Thanks," Detective Swanson replied.

Carlos unlocked the cell door, opened it, and stepped aside.

"Buzz me when you're ready to come out, Detective Swanson," Carlos said, and then he turned and walked away, returning to the security station.

As soon as Los Angeles County Homicide detective William Swanson crossed the threshold, the President of the Los Angeles County chapter of the Gloria Davis Fan Club, William Swanson, stepped into the cell.

"Ziz es private property," said a voice in the darkness.

Without windows, the bare light bulb imbedded in the ceiling behind metal mesh dimly cast shadows and shades of darkness, and it took a moment for William Swanson's eyes to adjust. When they did, he saw that the cell was painted in a faded, pale lavender hue, which Dr. Paul Prince would have informed, was clinically proven to induce calm.

William Swanson also saw the man he came to interview.

Adolph Von Bijou dressed in an orange prison jumpsuit stood erect with his back to the door, facing the back wall of the cell, sweeping his left arm up and down in a repetitious, vertical stroke; as if he held an invisible brush and he were painting an invisible column.

"Excuse me, sir, can I have a moment of your time?" the annoyingly persistent fan club president asked.

The old, bald Butler gestured as if he were setting down the invisible paint brush onto an invisible tray. He brushed the wrinkles from the formal black tie and tails uniform of his suit, and he turned around to face the young man standing on the sidewalk, beyond the wrought-iron gate.

"As I have zed to you before; Madam es not mentally fit to receive ze visitors," the director turned butler replied. "Madam es in ze bad state of ze mental decline, and es unfit for ze interviews."

"Actually, sir, it was *you* that I was hoping to interview," Detective William Swanson informed, stepping further into the cell, "I just have a few questions..."

♦ ♦ ♦ ♦ ♦ ♦ ♦ ♦ ♦ ♦ ♦ ♦

Twenty-eight minutes later, the buzzer sounded.

Sitting at the security monitors, Carlos, the guard, tapped the door-lock release button and looked up through the window into the hallway outside the high security cells, and he watched as Detective William Swanson stepped out of the psycho ward.

The detective's face reflected a slack expression of numb shock.

As he walked the short hallway and passed the small security station window, Detective Swanson lifted a slow hand wave toward the guard, and then, after the outer door was buzzed unlocked, he stepped out of the ward's exit.

It wasn't until almost eight minutes later that Carlos finally discovered the trail of blood that dripped along the tiled floor of the hallway, from door to door, right past the security window.

♦ ♦ ♦ ♦ ♦ ♦ ♦ ♦ ♦ ♦ ♦ ♦

In his office, sitting behind his desk shuffling through a stack of patient files, Dr. Paul Prince picked up the receiver of his telephone when it suddenly rang.

"Hello, this is Doctor Prin..." he began to say.

He was cut off by a frantically panicked voice.

"Señior Prince, this is Carlos, the guard, down in the high security ward. You better come down here quickly, sir, we've got a problem! It's that police detective that came in here! He's..."

"Calm down, and tell me what's happened," Dr. Prince

interrupted.

"Adolph Von Bijou has escaped! Detective Swanson is dead!" Carlos bellowed over the phone. "We don't know how he did it, how it could have happened, but Von Bijou somehow managed to get a hold of a butterknife! He attacked and killed the detective, and then he used the butterknife to remove the detective's face!"

Dr. Paul Prince gasped.

"Von Bijou used Detective Swanson's face to cover his own, and he walked right past us, out of the building! That madman's out there somewhere wandering around Hollywood right now, and we've got a dead body down here without a face!"

♦ ♦ ♦ ♦ ♦ ♦ ♦ ♦ ♦ ♦ ♦ ♦

Whatever routine that usually passed for 'normal' in an asylum was forgotten and forgone that day at The Matchabellini Institute within The Bel-Air Sanitarium.

Pandemonium and chaos ensued.

Many of the patient inmates became agitated and disruptive.

Some required sedation.

The guards were eventually forced to put the whole building into lockdown.

After the coroner left, things calmed down a bit.

And as soon as the faceless body was removed, Pepé, the janitor, went quickly to work mopping up the bloody mess and hosing down the gory aftermath splashed inside Adolph Von Bijou's vacant cell, softly humming *Hooray For Hollywood*, as he secretly harbored aspirations of making it big in Tinsel Town as a Glamour Guru to the Stars.

♦ ♦ ♦ ♦ ♦ ♦ ♦ ♦ ♦ ♦ ♦ ♦

≡ THE HEDDA HOPPER REPORT ≡

HOLLYWOOD, CALIFORNIA

IT'S THE END OF AN ERA FOR GLORIA DAVIS FANS AROUND THE WORLD AS DEMOLITION BEGINS THIS WEEK ON THE LONG-NEGLECTED MANSION IN WHICH THE RECLUSIVE SILENT SCREEN STAR AND SHOW BUSINESS LEGEND SPENT HER FINAL DAYS AFTER DECADES OUT OF THE PUBLIC EYE!

THE SCANDALIZED STAR BOUGHT THE SPRAWLING ESTATE AT THE HEIGHT OF HER ENORMOUS POPULARITY AND IT WAS, IN ITS DAY, ONE OF THE MOST OPULENT HOMES IN BEVERLEY HILLS. BUT OVER TIME THE PROPERTY WAS LEFT TO NEGLECT AND WAS, AFTER THE ACTRESS'S DEATH, CONDEMNED AND SOLD OFF TO AN INVESTMENT FIRM THAT RECENTLY ANNOUNCED PLANS TO ERECT LUXURY HI-RISE APARTMENTS AND CONDOMINIUMS AT THE LOCATION. BULLDOZERS WERE SPOTTED ARRIVING ON THE SUNSET BOULEVARD PROPERTY JUST THIS MORNING.

IN OTHER NEWS; WHILE IT'S LIKELY HE COULD HAVE ANY WOMAN HE DESIRES, ALL OF HOLLYWOOD SPECULATES ON WHICH LUCKY LADY MIGHT BECOME MRS. LIBERACE.

♦ ♦ ♦ ♦ ♦ ♦ ♦ ♦ ♦ ♦ ♦ ♦

There was a storm that night.

The final tour of the evening, the midnight departure of the MAP OF THE STARS bus, featuring a HOLLYWOOD HOMICIDES route for the more macabre-minded, was sold out.

Gloria Davis's mansion was still on the tour.

When the bus stopped in front of the estate, he stepped off the bus into the rain.

He waited for the Greyhound coach to pull away, and turn the corner, before turning to face the property. What he saw brought a tear to his eye.

The serpentine wrought-iron fence had been replaced

with chain-link. Beyond it, the land had been plowed and stripped. Where once there were overgrown trees and bushes that hid the bulk of the decrepit mansion, tractor gouges and dirt ridges now exposed a tilled field of mud and rock revealing the house to be in a state of excavation.

A bulldozer sat where a gazebo once stood.

The attic and third floor of the mansion itself had already been demolished and was completely toppled, leaving the floors and walls of the ground floor and second story exposed and open to the rain. The pipes of the Wurlitzer rose into the air beyond the demolition, appearing now stark against the sky like smokestacks and the remaining windows were shuttered with plywood.

He slipped through a breach in the chain-link fencing, and he stepped onto the property. Walking through the mud and debris, he had to step over the scattering of beams and post, arches and floorboards, which were now the broken and discarded bones of the dismantled beast that had been the mansion's majestic structure.

By the time he reached and was standing under what was left of the veranda, the black tie and tails of his uniform were rain soaked and dripping wet. He took a moment to shake out the wrinkles in his shirt and straighten the creases in his slacks, before taking in the view.

The rotting columns of the porch were askew; some were dismantled and leaning against what was left of the house. The front door was boarded; a CONDEMNED BY THE CITY sign was nailed to its exterior. Moss and mold covered the walls.

He was able to pull a loose board away from an entry hall window, gaining access to the interior of the house. He stepped onto a floor of shattered black and white marble tiles, and into a room draped in dusty webs, both spider and cob.

His decades of time spent in the dimness of 'The Dungeon' made it easy for his eyes to quickly adjust to the shadowy darkness on the inside of the house.

Rain poured into the mansion from demolition breaches

and compromises to the structure, and water cascaded down the grand staircase in a steady, rippling flow. Most of the furniture and furnishings had been removed, some remained crumbling where they always resided, covered in mold and webs.

Stepping carefully; he crossed the entry hall, and he entered the music room.

The room was in the disarrayed state of construction demolition. The oil-painted portrait of the great star had been removed, as had half of the wall on which it once hung. A tipped over couch, hemorrhaging its white cotton stuffing onto the wood-gouged floor, lay rain soaked in the corner of the room.

The wind blew a moan though the remaining bent pipes of the Wurlitzer organ.

He crossed the shadowy room, and stood before the keyboard.

The player's bench was designed with a hinged seat that could be raised to reveal its alternate purpose; as a lid for the shallow compartment meant for storing sheet music.

He bent and he opened the lid of the bench's trunk.

He removed the item stored inside the wooden seat.

Gloria Davis's missing hat box.

He removed the lid, and a fluff of cushioned cotton, and he gazed down upon the strip of bloody flesh and skin resting on a pillow of satin inside the hat box. The violently amputated and never before discovered sixteen year old face of Grendel Davodiannis, miraculously and mysterious preserved, over four decades after he had cut it off her head, late one night, on a soundstage, on the back lot at R. K. O. studios.

Setting aside the hat box, he held the chunk of facial flesh in his trembling hands, and he looked into her hauntingly beautiful eyes.

"Madam es as lovely as ever," Adolph Von Bijou admired. "You are ze greatest star in all ze universe!"

THE END

THE NAG

"True! – Nervous – Very, very dreadfully nervous I had been and am; but why *will* you say that I am mad? The disease had sharpened my senses – not destroyed – not dulled them. Above all was the sense of hearing acute. I heard all things in the heaven and in the earth. I heard many things in hell. How, then, am I mad? Harken! And observe how healthily – how calmly I can tell you the whole story..."

Excerpt from:
"THE TELL-TALE HEART" (pub. 1843)
EDGAR ALLAN POE

So, you think I'm insane.

And you claim this mental state is simply my attempt at building a legal defense.

That is madness, Detective Gabber.

For I have heard the tales corpses tell, and I've listened without lunacy.

I can assure you that I survived *this* tale with my sanity intact.

You shall see that all I say is true. You shall see that what I experienced is based in the solid foundations of reality, not fantasy conjured within a damaged or diseased mind. You will concur, by the conclusion of my statements, that I am as sane as any man who has ever witnessed the impossible and survived to warn the rest.

No need to shine a light in my eyes. Nor is there occasion to employ any of the other methods of harsh interrogation you and your fellow officers engage in, in your quest to persuade suspected 'Perps' into confessing their egregious acts, here in interrogation room # 4 at the homicide division of the City of Black Crow's fine and outstanding police department.

I am ready and prepared to tell you all that I know.

Consider this a true transcript of my voluntary and uncoerced confession.

I am here to confess that the strange and shocking events that occurred during the surreal hours after I killed my wife, earlier this very evening, are all real and true. I am here to confess that I have seen evidence of the supernatural realm that possessed her very soul.

So, without further ado, allow me to explain...

My name is Edgar Oldman, D.D.S. I am seventy-two years old. I retired from a very successful dental practice almost four years ago, after nearly four and a half decades of looking around inside other people's mouths and finding an income ample enough to provide a life of comfort and luxury. Born a non-practicing Catholic, I am in fairly good health, physically and mentally. I still hit the greens at least twice a month with my golfing buddies.

And yes, you heard me correctly; I killed my wife.

I first met Enora Louise Harper fifty-three years ago near the end of my senior year at a high school dance. We dated for eight years while I worked my way through college and medical school. After graduation, in the summer of 1974, she became Enora Louise Oldman. It was a small wedding with a handful of family and friends gathered at a church neither of us had ever attended.

Three years later we bought our home at the foot of Mount Diablo in the gated community of the Black Crow Country Club. After establishing myself in the medical community I opened my dental office twenty minutes away in downtown Walnut Creek and commuted in from the private Danville neighborhood each morning on the 680 freeway, returning each evening by way of the meandering San Ramon Valley Boulevard.

I won't bore you with the details of our dating or early married life, beyond my assurances that it was nothing extraordinarily special or unusual in nature. In fact, we had been married for several years before the realization occurred that I had married a nag.

Correction: a Nag with a capital **N**.

The oversight would be understandable to anyone who had seen us as a young couple all those years ago. I looked like the quintessential nerd. Sporting thick-rimmed glasses which sat upon an oversized schnozzle with protruding ears and a lazy eye, my parents could easily have named me Mortimer or Poindexter, and the name would have certainly fit.

Enora, on the other hand, radiated beauty.

Born a mix of Italian immigrants and Native American indigenous, Enora Louise Oldman (previously Harper) had raven black hair, piercing green eyes, and perfectly unblemished olive skin. Statuesque at nearly six feet in height. Regal in posture she exuded a physical beauty that demanded attention from all who observed her while capturing admiring glances from nearly all she encountered.

To see us side by side, *Lucky Bastard*, was an understandable summation.

And that's exactly how I felt.

At first.

Enora's extraordinary beauty blinded me to her (eventually) insufferable flaws.

After all, anyone could clearly see, I was lucky to have her.

But, over time, I saw her for how she really was; a downright, upright, first class, world class, four star, grade A, 100% Certified, aged in wood, grass-fed, homogenized and pasteurized, **NAG**!

And beware; her thoughts came from a factory that also processed nuts!

She bitched and complained in the morning, and she bitched and complained in the afternoon, and she bitched and complained in the evening. I would have bet my left nut and a pack of smokes she bitched and complained in her sleep, bitched and complained in her dreams.

From sun up to sun down, if she wasn't mocking me about one thing then she was criticizing me about another. She didn't like my family. She didn't like my hair. She didn't like my hobbies. She didn't like my breath. Her list of dislikes was endless. In the early days of our marriage I tried to please her. I changed my hair, I dropped my hobbies, I ate more mints, I even saw less of my family.

Happy wife, happy life, wasn't that what they always said?

So in the beginning I put a newlywedded effort into pleasing Enora. The effort ended when I realized that nothing would ever please her, *could* ever please her.

Her maiden name had been Harper and harping was her birthright.

Complaining was her comfort, discord her delight.

Yes she was a real witch.

A witch with a capital **B**.

If you get what I'm saying.

And for the next four decades all she did was nag me.

When I wanted to buy a sports car, she nagged me into buying an SUV. When I wanted to vacation on an African Safari, she nagged me into two weeks of sightseeing in Europe. When I wanted to put in a swimming pool, she nagged me into building a tennis court.

She nagged me about my job.

She nagged me about my drinking.

She nagged me about money.

She nagged me about chores.

She nagged me about everything, and she nagged me about nothing.

The clothes I wore, the way I spoke, my very existence; she approved of nothing, nada, none of it. And she had no trouble saying so. Every day, and in every way, she let me know she disapproved of everything about me.

"Edgar, why don't you wear contact lenses?"
"Edgar, why don't you stand up straight?"
"Edgar, why don't you act your age?"
"Edgar, why don't you behave this way?"
"Edgar, why don't you behave that way?"

Decade after decade, I listened to (and suffered through) her endless nagging!

"Edgar, when are you going to cut your hair?"
"Edgar, when are you going to cut the lawn?"
"Edgar, when are you going to take out the trash?"
"Edgar, when are you going to behave this way?"
"Edgar, when are you going to behave that way?"

I had come to realize, over agonizing time, that I had married a woman who had made it her mission in life to criticize my every move just as relentlessly as the shark from 'Jaws' pursued its next meal with teeth just as sharp. And when it came to standing up for myself or fighting back... well... I didn't have a bigger boat.

I can only be thankful I never had any children with that shrew of a woman.

Let me tell you about what she did to me once...

It happened just a few months after that dark abyss of unholy tethering I call our wedding day. We were invited to a private dinner at the home of the president of the California Division of the Dental Practitioners of America Association, at a swanky estate up in the hills of Berkeley overlooking the whole San Francisco Bay Area.

This invitation was quite an honor. How excited I was to be asked. I was so new in my dental practice, I thought it was a mistake. This was the type of invitation that was only ever bestowed upon the top doctors in the field. I was so nervous when the day finally arrived. I dressed in my best suit and tie.

Of course, Enora nagged me the whole way there.

The worst of it happened at dinner.

There we were Enora and I, two other dentists and

their wives, and our hosts; the top guy in our association and his wife, both of whom I'm desperately trying to impress.

At some point during dinner the wife of this Dental Association big shot asks me if I would like some ketchup, which was not out on the table, and I politely declined making a show of knowing the true origin of ketchup.

You see, the modern version of ketchup was invented by the French in 1845, during the great famine to mask the taste of burnt, badly prepared, or spoiling and rotting food, in order to make it somewhat palatable or acceptable to eat. It should never be necessary, or even considered, when enjoying a perfectly delicious meal such as the one our lovely hostess had prepared that fine evening. It would be an insult to the chef, and this magnificent meal, I reasoned, to slather ketchup all over the intended tastes and textures.

Well, no sooner had I finished this blatant 'kissing up' speech, when Enora looks up from her plate and loudly asks, "May I have some ketchup?"

I was mortified. I could have melted into my chair, I was so embarrassed.

And the thing you have to know is: Enora hated ketchup. She had always hated it.

She only did that to embarrass me. You have to know her to know that's true.

And wouldn't you know it, she nagged me about it on the way home.

"Edgar, how could you bore people with that stupid ketchup story?"

"Edgar, how could you eat so much of that awful meal?"

"Edgar, how could you associate with such people?"

"Edgar, how could you behave this way?"

"Edgar, how could you behave that way?"

Like I said, Detective Gabber, my wife Enora was a bitch with a capital **C**.

If you get what I'm saying.

In time, this was a fact that I had learned to just live with. Her nagging had beaten me down over the years. I learned to take it without ever fighting back. I was a broken man, a doormat. I was nothing more than her tongue's whipping boy.

But, all that changed tonight.

Tonight, I had had enough.

It all started while we were watching TV sitting up in bed, silently watching the six o'clock evening news. We decided to go to bed early as I had an early tee time on the course with some golfing buddies – I guess I won't be making that round this morning – and Enora said she wasn't feeling well and could use the rest.

Just before they were about to cover the sports news, Enora starts nagging me to go down to the kitchen and fix her a peanut butter and jelly sandwich. I told her I just wanted to catch the score of the Raiders game which I had missed earlier in the evening. I would be happy to go make her a PB&J sandwich right after, as soon as sports turned to weather.

This wasn't good enough for her.

"Edgar, I can't wait, I'm hungry now, why can't you do this for me?"

"Edgar, how can you just sit there, listening to my stomach growl?"

"Edgar, when will you..."

I finally just threw myself out of bed, grabbed a robe, and went down to the kitchen to shut her up. But even as I was fixing her a PB&J, I could hear her ranting and raving up in our bedroom, nagging me at the top of her lungs even as I was complying with her wishes.

I slapped the finished sandwich onto a paper plate, grabbed a napkin, and returned to our bedroom. She was yelling at me as I approached our bed, and when she took the paper plate from me, her voice took on a higher shrill.

"Edgar, how can you give this to me like this?"

"Edgar, why didn't you cut the crusts off, like I like?"

"Edgar, when are you going to listen to m..."

I turned from her nagging, left our bedroom, returned to the kitchen, retrieved the PB&J smeared butterknife from the sink, returned to our bedroom, and approached the bed.

When she held out the paper plate, I silently took the sandwich, cut off the edges (letting the crusts fall to the carpeted floor, making her gasp) and I tossed it back onto the paper plate, which she continued to hold out in front of her increasingly perplexed expression.

"Edgar, how could you..."

I reached out and slashed her throat with the PB&J smeared butterknife.

The dull knife was surprisingly efficient, just one swipe did it.

The slash was deep, from side to side, revealing muscle beneath skin.

Blood spurted into the air soaking the duvet, sheets, and blankets.

Enora's head rocked back onto her pillow, she dropped the paper plate to her lap.

A red fountain sprayed from severed arteries at decreasing heartbeat rhythms.

Even as she died, she nagged.

"Edgar... How... Could... You..."

Her words came out in bloody gurgles.

"Edgar..."

Watching her eyes slowly close felt triumphant.

The announcer on TV informed me; the Raiders also won that evening.

I thought that was the end of it.

I wrapped her up in the duvet, and dragged her into her palatial walk-in closet, with the intention of dealing with her body in the morning. I remade the bed with clean sheets and blankets from the linen pantry, and I climbed into bed just in time to watch Jeopardy.

Alex Trebek had just begun the double jeopardy round when it occurred to me that a PB&J sandwich sounded – inexplicably - pretty damn delicious to my tummy in that moment. I climbed out of bed and went down to the kitchen.

I was just licking the peanut butter from the butterknife (No! Not *that* butterknife! *That* butterknife was already in the dishwasher by that time) and getting ready to stick it into the jelly jar when I heard her.

Faintly, muffled, garbled: I *heard* her!

"Edgar, how could you do this to me?"

I dropped the butterknife into the sink.

I turned and left the kitchen with my heart pounding in my chest.

I climbed the stairs on shaky legs, sweaty palms clutching the banister.

I walked down the hall toward our bedroom with a lump in my throat.

I entered our bedroom hesitantly, and fearfully, yet compelled beyond my ability to turn away and flee. The door to her palatial walk-in closet remained closed, as I left it. I approached it slowly, straining to listen for sounds from within.

When I stood before it, I reached out and grasped the closet's door handle.

"EDGAR, WHY DID YOU DO THIS?!?!"

Shrill, shrieking, soul shredding; her voice was unmistakable.

I threw open the door to her closet and discovered Enora still lying on the floor, still wrapped in the duvet, still dead.

I approached her lifeless body, unwrapped the embroidered bedding from around her head, and I looked into her vacant eyes. The pupils stared off into a place beyond eternity, and the corneas were beginning to cloud over with a yellow, milky film.

Her mouth was closed, silent.

I believed in that moment that I surely must

have *imagined* her hateful voice still nagging me from beyond the grave. Perhaps this was a psychosomatic manifestation of the guilt I subconsciously must have felt over taking a life, I reasoned with myself.

I left her closet, leaving the duvet that still encased her body unwrapped from her head and exposing her face, and I returned to the bed we once shared. I was halfway through Wheel of Fortune – and more than halfway convinced that her phantom voice had just been a figment of my vivid imagination doing a little nagging of its own - when I remembered my forgotten, half-made, PB&J sandwich, sitting on the kitchen counter.

I climbed out of bed once more, and I was halfway down the stairs, my stomach beginning to rumble once more, when I heard her nagging voice again call out.

"Edgar, what were you thinking?!?!"

I raced back up the stairs, down the hall, and into our bedroom.

I threw open the door of her palatial walk-in closet, and entered.

Enora lay as silent and still as one would expect from the dead.

I truly wondered, in that moment, if I had gone crazy.

Exasperated, I took one of her silk scarves from its hanger and I wrapped it around Enora's head, again and again, covering her mouth as efficiently as a muzzle, tying it off at the back of her head with an aggressive knot.

"That ought to do it," I remember thinking.

How wrong I was.

I returned to the kitchen, I ate the PB&J over the sink.

I returned to our bedroom, returned to our bed.

I watched an endless array of unfunny sitcoms and contrived dramas.

Two hours passed when nothing broke the silence except the television.

I was once again on the verge of having fully convinced myself that it was all just guilt-induced imagination, exasperated by exhaustion, when she shrieked out once more.

"Edgar, how could you do this?"

A barrage of nagging ensued.

"Edgar, why would you do this?"

I threw back the covers, and flew out of bed.

"Edgar, what were you thinking?"

I ran across the bedroom to the door of her palatial walk-in closet.

"Edgar, when are you going to turn yourself in?"

I threw open the closet door.

"Edgar, you've really done it this time!"

Enora still lay on the floor of her palatial walk-in closet, eyes staring vacantly.

"Edgar..."

The silk scarf still covered her mouth.

"...I'm going to tell everyone..."

Her voice was coming from the slash in her neck.

"...what you did!"

The fleshy edges of the open wound curled back to form crude, jagged lips, and her head lolled back on slack muscles as the blood-coagulating gash in her throat opened and closed in taunting articulation.

"EDGAR, YOU'LL GET THE ELECTRIC CHAIR!" screamed the open cut.

I nearly screamed myself. If there was ever a moment when my sanity was truly in question, it was surely that moment, Detective Gabber. But even as my mind struggled to understand what I was seeing, she nagged, taunted and confused me.

The bloody lips of the gash smacked together loudly.

"I taste peanut butter!" SMACK SMACK *"Couldn't you have at least cleaned off the knife before you killed me with it, Edgar?"*

I stammered to answer, then stopped myself. This couldn't be happening.

"Now you've done it, Edgar," the open wound taunted, drooling blood, *"they're gonna give you the death penalty!!!"*

A strip of flesh flopped out of the bloody wound and slid across the opening as if it were a slick tongue, licking its lips, before disappearing back into the dripping gash.

That did it.

I screamed.

I couldn't help it!

"That's it, Edgar! Wake the neighbors! Let's get the police out here!"

Enora's voice gargled out of the jagged slash as if she were speaking underwater.

I staggered backward away from the corpse with the mocking and taunting death wound slashed across her throat like a necklace.

As I slammed the closet door shut, I saw the slit form a smile.

"You're gonna fry, Edgar! You're gonna fry!" it screamed from inside the closet.

My mind reeled as I ran from the bedroom, ran from her nagging voice.

"Edgar, why did you..."

I couldn't get far enough away.

"Edgar, how could you..."

Past the kitchen, past the front room, past her knitting room and my home office, I was all the way out in the garage before I was far enough away to no longer hear her hateful nagging. I paced the cement floor between her Chevy and my Ford, trying to think up a plan.

You have to understand, at that point, I was likely in shock by what I had just witnessed. I wasn't thinking clearly. Nothing about what happened next played out the way I intended. I was just trying to figure out what my next move should be.

I looked at the drills and saws hooked up on the wall over my workbench.

I considered dismantling her, to silence her.

But even with my medical background, I knew this to be a task too gruesome to consider. True, I had just cut her throat but that was an act of passion, a loss of impulse control. I didn't mean to do it, I simply lashed out. I hadn't thought about it, it just happened.

But the preconceived notion and idea of purposefully taking a chainsaw to her limbs, and removing her arms and legs, or cutting off her head with an ax or a hacksaw was beyond repugnant to my sensibilities. I shuddered at the thought.

No, that was out of the question.

I continued to pace between the cars, considering without a revelation, trying to think up a plan, trying not to panic, failing with both. It was slightly after midnight when I left the garage and reentered the house without a clue as to what my next move would or should be.

As soon as I stepped inside, I could hear her voice coming from upstairs.

She was still screaming, she was still raving, and she was still nagging.

"Edgar, look at how much of my blood you got all over the carpet!"

As I passed through the kitchen, something compelled me to grab the butterknife from out of the sink. As I climbed the stairs, her spectral nagging grew louder.

"Edgar, I'm gonna start stinking up the closet if you don't get in here and deal with me!"

I entered our bedroom, suddenly aware that I was holding the butterknife out in front of me, like a weapon.

"Edgar..."

NAG! – NAG! – NAG!

I snapped.

I ran to the door of her palatial walk-in closet and

flung it open.

Raising the butterknife up high, I threw myself at her.

I stabbed her. Then I stabbed her again.

Over and over, I stabbed her.

Again and again, I stabbed her.

I was out of control, Hell-bent on silencing her.

I stabbed her in the throat.

I stabbed her in the face.

I stabbed her in the eyes.

I stabbed the lumpy length of her body, through the fabric of the rolled up duvet, dozens - if not hundreds - of times, grunting like a savage animal with every thrust of the knife.

My mind left my body and I blacked out. I felt as if I were floating outside of myself. If the slash in her throat still spoke, I could no longer hear it; a high-pitched buzzing rang between my ears. My vision began to dim. Leaving the knife in her chest, I pushed myself away.

I staggered out of the closet, away from my tormentor, before losing consciousness and falling to the floor in a black, dreamless void.

I awoke to a choir of Enora's voices screaming in multi-tonal chorus:

"EDGAR, HOW COULD YOU..." "EDGAR, WHY WOULD YOU..." "EDGAR..."

"EDGAR..." "EDGAR..." "EDGAR..." "EDGAR, YOU'RE SO..." "EDGAR..." "ED"

"GAR" "EDGAR..." "EDGAR, WHEN WILL YOU..." "EDGAR..." "EDGAR..."

"EDGAR..." "EDGAR..." "EDGAR..." "EDGAR, HOW CAN YOU..." "EDGAR..."

"EDGAR, WHY CAN'T YOU..." "EDGAR..." "EDGAR, IF YOU

WEREN'T SO..."

I ran into the palatial walk-in closet, screaming; "SHUT UP! SHUT UP!"

I pulled the duvet away from her, exposing a body riddled with stab wounds.

What I saw felt like a shocking slap in the face.

The best way I can describe it, Detective Gabber, is to tell you about the time I was employed at a pet supply shop when I was working my way through medical school. From time to time, the goldfish would jump out of the tanks and whenever we discovered one on the floor, if it wasn't already dead, it would be found with its little mouth opening and closing, as it struggled to take oxygen into its gills.

The stab wounds on Enora's body gasped and gulped just like those little mouths.

Opening and closing, all up and down her arms and legs, head and torso; the vile, bloody holes in her flesh screamed out her hateful messages of nagging in a shrill, overlapping cacophony of accusatory rants.

"EDGAR, WHY CAN'T YOU..." "EDGAR..." "EDGAR, IF YOU WEREN'T SO..."

"EDGAR..." "EDGAR, HOW COULD YOU..." "EDGAR, WHY WOULD YOU..."

"EDGAR, HOW CAN YOU..." "EDGAR..." "EDGAR..." "EDGAR..." "EDGAR..."

It rang in my ears like ice picks stabbing into my brain.

When I noticed the wound in her chest - which still held the incriminating butterknife - sputtering and snapping, as if it were trying to spit out the silver eating utensil jammed to the hilt within it, I lost all control. I screamed.

It was around this time, Detective Gabber, when your colleagues here at the Danville P.D. arrived to see what all the fuss was about. I suppose my neighbors....

Ah, an interruption to my confession!

Detective Muir-

Welcome-

Won't you join us here in interrogation room # 4.

You look as if you've seen a ghost!

Of course I'll give you and Detective Gabber a moment to converse.

"I'm sorry to interrupt, Detective Gabber," Detective Muir said, his voice a shaky whisper, "but I think you need to come down to the morgue."

"I'm kind of busy, right now," Detective Gabber replied, "I'm conducting an interview, here. Mister Oldman has just confessed to murdering his wife this evening and I..."

"Yeah, I know, I've heard the whole story," Detective Muir interrupted, "that's why I think you better come down to the morgue with me."

Detective Gabber looked away from me and glared at his colleague.

"What the hell's going on?" my inquisitor inquired.

Detective Muir cleared his throat and wiped the sweat from his upper lip.

"We've taken a statement from the victim," Detective Muir said.

Detective Gabber's mouth dropped open.

"You've taken a statement from the *murder* victim?" Detective Gabber asked.

"Yes," Detective Muir replied, his eyes widening. Then he took a deep breath and let it all out. "I couldn't believe it either! I'm still not sure I do! They brought her in on a gurney, and as soon as they unzipped the body bag, she started ranting and raving! She told us the whole story! You just have to come down to the morgue and see this for yourself! You're not going to believe what she's using to talk with! I mean where the voices are coming from! Officer Rucker fainted when he saw it! You're just going to have to come down to the morgue and see it for yourself! I'm still not sure *I* even believe it!"

"Let me get this straight, Detective Muir, are you trying to tell me that the *murder victim* has filed a report?" Detective Gabber asked.

Detective Muir shuddered.

"Well, to tell you the truth," Detective Muir whispered, "she's really just kind of harping about the whole thing, actually. *Officer, when are you going to do this! Officer, when are you going to do that!* I'd call it less 'making a report' and more like just plain 'nagging' if you ask me."

When Detective Gabber returned his attention toward me, the expression on his face, the look in his eyes, confirmed that his mind reeled with confusion and mounting terror.

I smiled.

If this tale reflects a compromised mental state ...

If insanity inspires my confession...

Welcome to my madness!

THE END

TWO HEADS ARE BETTER THAN ONE

Anna Rigley whistled as she showered, hummed as she brushed her teeth, and danced as she dressed that morning as she prepared for her day at work. Standing in her bathroom applying a dab of lipstick while trying not to smile, she looked at her glowing image in the mirror, and was overcome with joy.

She glanced at her watch: 6:45 am. Just eight hours and fifteen minutes until her first pre-natal appointment and the confirmation of the pending blessed event to which she first became aware just last weekend, in this very bathroom.

Anna had taken the home pregnancy test this past Sunday afternoon while her husband divided his attention between the game on TV (the Oakland A's vs. the Mariners in Seattle) and work emails on his phone (he was on the legal team of one of his firm's biggest clients, and presenting opening statements in court next week), when she came running in waving the test stick in the air like a winning lottery ticket.

They held each other, laughing and dancing, all through the second inning.

They knew exactly when it happened. Last month when his company rented that fancy hotel in Napa during their Executive's Retreat. On the last night after the awards dinner with drinking and dancing; they made love on the fur rug by the fireplace in their room. They were both sure this is when it happened.

She had to wait a whole month to get an appointment with one of the doctors down at the Los San Leandros Family Planning Clinic & Birthing Center and, finally, this afternoon, at

3pm, she was scheduled to meet with Dr. Hasslein to make sure everything was going as it should, and to get her first glimpse at the little life that was now growing inside her.

She didn't know what to expect, she had never really paid much attention when other women showed off their sonogram pictures and she wasn't sure what she would be able to see this early into the pregnancy. Would she see arms and legs? Fingers and toes? Would she, perhaps, see a little pea-sized head? A face?

She didn't know what to expect, but she was excited to get through her day at work to get to her appointment. Then she would get her first miraculous glimpse of the child she now joyfully carried in the cradle of her womb.

Anna hugged her belly as she walked down the stairs, from the bedroom to the kitchen. She kissed her husband twice - right on the lips - as she rushed out the door, then she practically skipped to her car parked in the driveway.

Is it gross to carry the positive home pregnancy test stick with me in a baggie in my purse? she wondered, as she backed the car down the driveway and out into the street. *I did rinse it off pretty well.*

She watched as the little house she shared with her husband – the first home of their expanding family – retreated in the rearview mirror.

Perhaps it's a little gross, keeping the stick I peed on, but she didn't care. She was too happy. She was proud of that little red + on the handle. It represented the best news she had ever received.

Anna stopped at Starbucks on the way to work that morning. She had done her research on caffeine and she decided that she would still allow herself one cup each morning until the fourth month and then she would quit – cold turkey – until after the baby was born.

She placed her usual order – a Grande Carmel Macchiato – and then she stepped away from the counter and waited for her name to be called.

She listened with interest to the other names that were called before hers, and she scanned the name tags of the employees behind the counter. Eventually, her name was called and as she reached over the counter and took her coffee she took note of the barista's name tag: Lindsey.

Oh, that's a nice name, she thought.

Anna had been thinking about names lately. She was currently considering Peggy and Penny for a girl, and Donny and Denny if she had a boy. Now Lindsey was in the running. She had already gone through hundreds of names in her mind since last Sunday. Dozens considered and eliminated. David? Sheila? Robert? Whitney? Joseph? Sarah? Kyle? There was plenty of time to decide.

She returned to her car with the coffee, and she drove to her office. She parked in her designated spot, and she entered the towering international corporate headquarters of The Conglomerated Chemical Company.

"Well, don't you look especially happy and glowing this morning, Miss Anna," said Hank, the building's security guard, as she crossed the lobby to the elevators.

"It's a beautiful morning, Hank," she replied coyly, having previously decided that it was too soon to share the good news with co-workers and other acquaintances.

"Tis, indeed! Tis, indeed!" he agreed.

As she rode the elevator to the sixteenth floor, alone in the confined space, she hummed the melody to the song *her* mother sang to her when *she* was a baby:

ROCK-A-BYE BABY,
ON THE TREE TOPS,
WHEN THE WIND BLOWS,
THE CRADLE WILL ROCK,
WHEN THE BOUGH BREAKS,
THE CRADLE WILL FALL,
AND DOWN WILL COME BABY,
CRADLE AND ALL…

Her smile faltered. She had never before considered the dark and ominous words to that lullaby. How inappropriate that song actually was to sing to children nestled in their beds anticipating sleep.

As she stepped off the elevator, she shrugged off the dark and ominous omen choosing to focus instead on the miraculous life growing inside her belly. By the time she reached the door of her office at the end of the hallway her excitement had returned to its full level of anticipation.

Anna entered her office, closed the door, sat behind her desk, and looked at her watch: 7:52 am. A little over seven hours to go...

Can't wait! her mind squealed. She had no idea how she was ever going to get through this day, or get any work done when all she could think about was her appointment at the obstetrician's office and the sonogram she would be having this afternoon.

Hope everything's okay! was the thought she tried not to think. Early in the marriage, there had been a miscarriage and then came a reluctant abortion on the second attempt. The sonogram on their last attempt had revealed unmanageable deformities. These would have created lifelong challenges that could prove insurmountable to the poor child burdened with a life too difficult to survive. Anna nearly lost her mind within the subsequent depression and despair.

This time it's different, she thought desperately embracing the belief without reason or cause, pushing negative thoughts away simply out of fear they may help to create a negative reality. *I just need to keep a level head on my shoulders!*

"Just keep a level head," she murmured aloud.

She anticipated the hands of the clock to move slowly that morning but surprisingly lunchtime came quickly, and with it came a deep rumbling of hunger of which she had never before endured.

I'm starved! she thought with little exaggeration.

Anna ate a full ham sandwich, along with a salad and a cup of vegetable soup, topped off with a chocolate chip cookie while sitting alone in the cafeteria.

It was 'Bring Your Child to Work' day, and the large seating area of the dining room was filled with children eating lunch with their parents. Anna's co-workers were either passing acquaintances or strangers, as it was a large company and nearly impossible to know everybody.

She watched the children intently; hardly able to believe that she and her husband would soon have one of their own. She placed her hands against her abdomen, and she wondered if it was a boy or a girl that grew inside her, if she carried a son or a daughter.

I'll be happy either way!

As long as everything goes as it should this time.

Anna finished her lunch, discarded the tray, and exited the cafeteria.

"Keep a level head on your shoulders, Anna," she murmured again.

She spent the remainder of the afternoon in meetings, and that helped to keep her mind focused on her work. She was surprised when she returned to her office that it was already 2:00 pm. She spent that last half hour at work sitting at her desk simply staring at the clock fantasizing about being a mother, and waiting until she could leave at 2:30pm for her obstetrician appointment.

When her workday was over, she closed up her office and she took the elevator down to the lobby. She said "good night" to Hank, the security guard, as she left the building. She climbed into her car and she backed it out of its designated parking spot. She drove across town and a few minutes later she pulled into the parking lot of the Los San Leandros Family Planning Clinic & Birthing Center.

She was a few minutes early, but she bolted from the car as if she were late. She moved quickly and her smile was broad as she entered the medical facility.

She approached the front counter and the receptionist sitting behind the window gave her a clipboard of forms to fill out, and directed her to the second floor waiting room.

When she reached the second floor, she found a room filled with women in varying stages of pregnancy waiting as they sat on a scattering of benches and chairs. She took her place among them. She began to fill out the new patient paperwork as the sound of an unseen baby began to cry from some other room in the building.

Periodically, a friendly-looking nurse with short red hair came out from the back rooms to call out a patient name and then take the responding woman back into an examination room.

It wasn't long before the red-headed nurse called out: "Anna Rigley?"

"Right here," Anna replied, as she rose from her chair.

She could feel the eyes of the other waiting women on her as she crossed the room. She handed the clipboard of forms to the nurse who took them with a smile.

"Just down the hall, last door on the left," the red-headed nurse directed, "exam room # 2."

When they were behind the closed door of exam room # 2, the red-headed nurse motioned for Anna to take a seat on the examination table.

"My name is Jackie, I'm Dr. Hasslein's medical assistant and lab tech," the red-headed nurse explained. "I'm going to administer the sonogram and then Dr. Hasslein will go over the pictures with you before conducting his exam at which time we'll need you in the stirrups. But for now, you can just lay back with your legs out in front of you on the table and I'll prep you for the sonogram. Any questions before we get going?"

"A million, but none right now," Anna giggled, "I'm just so excited!"

"I haven't met an expectant mother who wasn't," Jackie the nurse replied, good-naturedly. "I'll step out of the room so you can put on this gown – it opens in the back - and then we'll get our first look at your baby."

The medical assistant stepped out of the room. Anna changed into the paper gown. Jackie the nurse returned.

"Just lie back and relax," Jackie the nurse instructed. "I'm applying a liberal coating of the conduction jelly to your belly and onto the scanner pad so we can slide it around freely and get a good look at what's going on inside you."

Anna shivered as the jelly was cold as ice. With the sudden sting of the scanner pad touching her belly, the dark and ominous words of the lullaby her mother had sung to her when she was a child returned and invaded her thoughts:

ROCK-A-BYE BABY...

The medical assistant turned on the sonogram, next to the examination table, and a static-filled screen came to life.

ON THE TREE TOPS...

The nurse moved the scanner pad across her belly and the screen changed to a black and white image of an organized static that Anna instantly and instinctively knew to be a view into her reproductive system.

WHEN THE WIND BLOWS...

As Jackie the red-headed nurse moved the scanner pad, the image on the screen changed, altered, clarified.

THE CRADLE WILL ROCK...

A shape began to define an outline within the jumbled static of the indeterminate mass; a human form, small and fleeting, appeared on the screen.

WHEN THE BOUGH BREAKS...

A tiny torso, with little arms and legs, suddenly appeared in the jumble.

THE CRADLE WILL FALL...

The medical assistant adjusted the depth-degree distance on the monitor, and the screen zoomed in on the two small heads, growing side-by-side, atop the tiny shoulders of the fetus living inside of Anna Rigley.

AND DOWN WILL COME BABY...

Jackie the nurse took one look at the two-headed baby and screamed. She stood up, and she fainted, hitting the linoleum-tiled floor face first.

CRADLE AND ALL...

Anna was left stunned and speechless as chaos ensued.

Nurses, interns, and orderlies came rushing in and out of exam room # 2.

Doctors came inquiring as a commotion developed around the sonogram monitor.

Jackie the nurse was revived, and taken out on a stretcher.

Dr. Hasslein appeared and cleared the room.

When it was just the two of them, Anna listened in stunned silence as Dr. Hasslein – who never once looked her directly in her eyes - spoke a lot of medical mumbo-jumbo that amounted to "we can't help you, you need to see a specialist."

He gave her a black and white printout photograph of a sonogram image that clearly displayed the two heads of the tiny fetus growing inside her womb.

An offer of a glass of water was the only other display of concern given before she was left alone in exam room # 2 to change back into her street clothes in preparation of her departure from the Los San Leandros Family Planning Clinic & Birthing Center.

As she crossed the waiting room filled with women in varying stages of pregnancy, she noticed the front desk receptionist *specifically* did not make eye contact with her, and Jackie the red-headed nurse was nowhere in sight.

Anna ran across the parking lot of the Los San Leandros

Family Planning Clinic & Birthing Center to her car with tears in her eyes. She fell into the driver's seat with a moan of despair. Her hand shook as she inserted the car's key into the ignition slot.

She drove home in a state of shock.

She pulled the car into the driveway, cut the engine, and then she sat in silence behind the wheel thinking about what had just happened. After a few minutes, she exited the car, and she went into the house. As she closed the front door, her husband came bounding down the stairs to greet her.

"How did it go?" asked Scott, the head that sat on her husband's right shoulder.

"You look upset," said Sam, the head that sat on her husband's left shoulder.

"It went okay, I guess," Anna replied. "I was just left in shock over how unprofessional they were there. You'd think all they ever saw there was the same usual-looking babies women keep giving birth to. Their reaction just left me speechless."

"You can't keep letting other people's prejudices bother you," replied Sam, the head that sat on her husband's left shoulder.

"We've gotten used to it," added Scott, the head that sat on her husband's right shoulder.

"I know, you're right," Anna conceded, with a smile.

She kissed her husband – twice, right on the lips – as she set down her purse.

"It's just that people can be so frustrating," she added.

He took her into his arms.

"We're here for you," Scott said.

"Have you thought anymore about names?" Sam asked.

"I'm leaning toward Donny and Denny if it's a boy and Peggy and Penny for a girl," she replied.

"Those are great names," said Sam.

"How are you feeling otherwise?" asked Scott.

Anna thought about it for a moment.

"I'd say ..." she considered her words "...I kept a level head on my shoulders."

"That's great," Scott exclaimed.

"We're proud of you," Sam added.

"And keeping a level head on my shoulders is not easy these days," Anna lamented, "I really struggle with it."

"That goes double for me," Sam replied.

"Ditto," Scott agreed.

Anna smiled.

"Hey, I just thought of something," Sam pondered, "what if it's one of each?"

"A boy *and* a girl? Scott wondered.

Anna stared at her husband with a look of bewilderment equal to the expression of shock she wore at the Los San Leandros Family Planning Clinic & Birthing Center.

After a moment, they fell back into each other's arms laughing their heads off.

THE END

UNDER THE BED

My name is Tommy.
I'm this many.
You can't see em in the dark, but I'm holding up four fingers.
Next year, I'll be a whole hand.
I got sent to bed with no desert.
I cried about it, but Mommy still said "GO."
Mommy got mad because I wrote my name on the wall.
She said she's proud of me cause I can write my name, but she's mad it's on the wall.
I can kinda see it right now, even in the dark, over by my closet door, cause of R2-D2.
I did it with my crayons, a different color for each letter:

TOMMY

I still got to eat pasghetti and meatballs,
But when dinner was over, that was it.
"Go to bed, no desert," Mommy said. "Now."
So here I am in bed, in trouble, in the dark.
But now I can smell the brownies, so I'm gonna try crying again.
I can do it any time I want, watch...
See...
I got the tears going pretty good, and pretty soon I saw the shadows of her feet in the light shining in from the crack under the door, as she stood in the hall, just outside my room.
She did not come in.
"Quiet down," I heard her say, "don't make me come in there."
She sounded mad.
The shadow feet under the door walked away

I gave up crying.
When Mommy gets mad, I get scared!
Even Daddy said he was afraid of Mommy's madness when I sneak listened to him talking on the phone one day to *his* mommy, my Nana Banana.
Nana Banana's real name is Velma but she doesn't like to be called that.
She always smells like cookies.
My daddy's on a Busy Nest Trip.
He goes on Busy Nest Trips all the time.
I heard Mommy telling *her* Mommy that she was happy for the breaks.
She just wants to be called Grandmother Louise.
She always smells like the stinky red Kool-Aid she drinks in the funny little glasses that I can never get to have a sip of.
My tummy rumbled for the brownies I smelled, but sleepiness got in me too.
I closed my eyes for a second, but I didn't want to go to sleep.
But I think I did.
Then I sat up in the dark, afraid!
It seemed later than it was before.
The light in the hall was off; the crack under the door was dark.
The only light was the R2-D2 nightlight by my closet door showing TOMMY on the wall.
Rain was now hitting my bedroom window.
It didn't smell like brownies anymore.
I looked around my bedroom, but my eyes just saw dark.
The tall light on a pole by the street put tree shadows on my window that looked scary.
Branch arms and stick fingers waved at me in the wind.
They reached for me like claws scratching at my bedroom window.
Then a sound.
SHHHHHH...like someone shushing in a whisper.
I pulled my Lion King blankets up around me tight.
I didn't want to cry, but I did a little bit.

I was thinking about running to Mommy's room.

I was just about to put my feet on the floor when I heard something move under the bed.

Something made a scratching sound.

Some… thing.

SHHHHHH… a little bit louder.

And for sure coming from under the bed.

"Mommy!" I cried out in the dark.

The thing under the bed stopped still.

I think it was listening.

I could hear it breathing.

SHHHHHH…

"Mooooommmmmmmy!" crying made it hard to scream.

The light in the hall came on shining in through the crack under the door.

Footsteps coming, then shadow feet just outside my room.

She threw open my bedroom door.

With the hall light shining behind her, she was an outline of darkness.

I learned about outlines when I traced my hand to draw a turkey for Thanksgiving.

I couldn't see her face, I couldn't see her eyes.

I could just see her outline; black darkness like my turkey hand.

"What did I tell you?" she whispered like the snake's hiss from Jungle Book.

"But… I… heard…. somethi…" crying hiccups tangled my mouth.

"You heard the rain, go to sleep," she hisspered.

"But…" hiccup.

"If I have to come in there, you're in big trouble."

"But…" hiccup.

"Don't make me tell you again!"

She closed the door.

Her footsteps walked away.

The hall light went dark through the crack under the door.

Darkness filled my bedroom, filled my eyes.

Even R2-D2 didn't seem as bright.
My ears tried to hear past the sound of the rain, but that's all I heard; rain.
I settled down deep into my bed with the Lion King blankets up high under my chin.
The tall light, on a pole, out by the street, kept shining the scary tree puppet show on my window blinds and...
Something moved under the bed.
A sound like claws scrapping the wood floorboards put chills on my arm hairs.
I pulled the Lion King blankets up over my head.
It smelled like meatball farts, but I felt safer, under the covers.
My heart was beating as fast as Mr. Cotton Ears, our pet rabbit.
Dad says that Mr. Cotton Ears' heart beats so fast because of his 'Moetabulizum'.
Dad says that Mr. Cotton Ears' 'Moetabulizum' runs fast, but our 'Moetabulizum' runs slow and that if we...
Another scraping movement, another shifting sound.
Something, for sure, was under the bed.
I tried not to think about it.
I tried to think about something else.
I remembered our trip to Disneyland last year.
It was the first and only time I flew in a airplane.
There was a baby who cried the whole way there, but I was good.
I didn't cry once. The whole trip.
I got to meet Mickey Mouse!
We went on Splash Mountain and Small World.
We saw Robot Pirates on a boat ride.
The Pirates were fake people called 'Animal Tronics'.
I still remember the song they sang.
"Yo Ho, Yo Ho..."
*SHHHHHH...*a whispering hiss from under the bed.
I poked my head out from under the Lion King blankets.
"Moooooommmmmmmy!" I cried out in the dark.
*SHHHHHH...*the loudest hush of all.
It stopped me from crying out for Mommy again.

I sat up tall and stiff listening.
Straining to listen, all I heard was the sound of the rain.
Or maybe I heard some*thing* else.
"Is someone there?" I whispered.
SHHHHHHHHHHHHHHHHHHHHHHHHHHHHHHHHHHHHHHH-HHH!
Long. Slow. Low. Hissing like the Jungle Book snake.
My eyes burned tears.
My lips trembled.
My body shook.
I tried to hold it in, but I exploded...
"MOOOOOOOMMMMMMMMY!!!" I screamed.
The thing under the bed shifted angrily, then settled.
Light blinked on through the crack under the door.
Footstep sounds, then shadow feet approaching.
The door flew open.
She stood in the hall like a black outline.
Face unseen, eyes unseen. Darkness against the light.
"What did I tell you? Do I have to come in there?"
Anger made her voice strange.
"If I have to come in there, you're in big trouble."
She stood still, and I trembled.
"But... Mommy..." I whispered small.
"Don't make me say it again!"
She closed the door.
Footsteps faded away.
The light in the hall shining through the crack under the door went dark.
I settled my head back onto my pillow.
I pulled the Lion King blankets up to my chin.
I closed my eyes, and then opened them again, over and over.
The darkness was the same either way.
I took a deep breath and told myself that there was nothing under the bed.
No *thing*!
I listened again, and found the rain had stopped.

It was quieter than quiet.

Darker than dark.

Okay...

I'll tell the truth...

I did cry *a little bit* on the Pirates ride.

Come to think of it....

The fake people there were kinda spooky.

They had shinier eyes, and rubbery skin.

They moved like plastic people.

Almost like real people, but...

Fake!

Maybe this isn't the best thing to think about when you're in the dark afraid!

Fake people aren't real.

Maybe I should think about...

Another sound.

Shifting. Scraping.

Something under the bed moving.

I sat up and leaned over the side of the bed.

By moonlight, I could just barely see the floorboards as I looked down the side of the bed.

I looked away, afraid I would see something crawl out from under the bed.

Some *thing*!

Almost in a panic, needing to see in the dark, I reached out to turn on the lamp sitting on the nightstand and something grabbed my wrist in the dark.

I screamed.

I pulled my arm free from whatever held it.

The hall light came on, shining in through the crack at the bottom of the bedroom door.

I leaned over the side of the bed and grabbed the bottom edge of the blankets.

Footsteps echoed in the hall, approaching my bedroom door.

I pulled up the blankets that dangled to the floor and I was just about to look under the bed as the knob on my bedroom door

began to turn.
As I was about to look under the bed, as I was about to see what lurked there, I paused.
I looked over to the R2-D2 nightlight.
The crayon writing on the wall had been changed. It no longer spelled out:

TOMMY

The crayon writing on the wall now said:

MOMMY

I looked under the bed.
My mommy was hiding there.
SHHHHHH… she hushed.
Fear was in her eyes.
"Don't make her come in here again," Mommy whispered, hissing like the Jungle Book snake. "If she has to come in here, we're in big trouble."
I didn't understand what I was seeing…
If it had been Mommy hiding under the bed this whole time then who…
My bedroom door flew open, and she stood there in the hall just as she had moments earlier.
I couldn't see her face, I couldn't see her eyes.
She was an outline of darkness.
And she came into my room.

THE END

BOO!

"BOO!"

The baby giggled.

The old woman dressed as a witch smiled.

"Isn't he just a little angel," she exclaimed as she covered her eyes behind the wrinkled palms of her age-spotted hands, once more.

"PEAK... A..." the old woman nearly sang.

The baby's young mother shifted uncomfortably in her seat. Once again she glanced around the crowded bus for a vacant seat to which she could move, finding none. As it was late in the afternoon on Halloween day, there were several werewolves, vampires, and witches riding the old Greyhound as it navigated the rainy and foggy city streets. The bus was filled to capacity with costumed characters dressed for an evening of trick or treating.

"BOO!" the old woman cackled, once again, as she lowered her hands from her eyes.

The baby, dressed in a little vampire outfit, giggled less enthusiastically, and then yawned.

"Thank you, but he's not always an angel," the young mother sighed, adjusting the cape of her own vampire attire to partially cover the baby in her lap. "In fact, he's just started teething, and can get quite crabby. So like I said, maybe he should get some rest now..."

The old woman, ignoring the young mother, replaced her wrinkled hands over her eyes.

"PEAK... A... BOO!" the old woman repeated, and the pointy black hat with the bright yellow moon embroidered on the front and stars on the brim fell askew on her head as she removed her hands from her eyes. She quickly adjusted it, grunting to clear her throat.

The baby giggled, yet he looked slightly annoyed.

Rain and wind battered the exterior of the old Greyhound with a cold winter bluster, but inside the bus it was a steaming sauna of stranger's breath and body heat. The young mother attempted to slightly lower the window beside which she sat, failing to do anything more than drip wet condensation from the foggy glass onto the armrest of her chair. The window pane would not budge even a merciful fraction of an inch.

"Goo, Goo, Goo," the old woman's 'baby talk' sounded like a thick phlegmy growl, and she finished it with a hack and a cough. "All my grandchildren are grown now," she said, clearing her throat once more.

The baby raised a fussy sound.

"I think he's getting tired," the young mother repeated.

"PEAK..." the age spotted hands returned to her face, recovering her eyes.

The young mother sighed.

"...A..." the old woman drew the syllable out like she was gargling a lullaby.

The baby frowned.

"...BOO!" the old woman nearly shrieked like a hag at her cauldron.

The baby started to cry as the old woman lowered her hands and uncovered her eyes.

The Greyhound pulled over at a bus stop. Passengers stepped off the bus as others stepped on in ghoulish or whimsical costumes. It was standing room only by the time the bus pulled back out into traffic once more leaving the young mother without the option of changing seats, and trapped against the steamy window as the old woman occupied the aisle seat.

"Boop, Boop, Boop," the old woman croaked, and she gently tapped the baby's nose with a shriveled fingertip as she expelled each *Boop*.

The baby responded by increasing the volume of his cry.

"I don't think he likes tha...," the young mother began to explain.

"PEAK," the old woman ignored and interrupted the young mother of the baby who held her attention as she replaced her wrinkled hands over her eyes blinding herself behind pale white palms, once more.

"I don't mean to be rude, but...," the young mother sighed.

"...AAAAAA...," the old woman continued louder.

The young mother squeezed her eyes closed in frustration. She wearily opened them again when she heard the old witch finish her repetition.

"BOO!" the old woman cackled smiling.

The baby, whose cries had died down to whimpering snivels, also sort of smiled.

Somewhere in the back of the bus a mummy sneezed, tearing off a strand of his costume into which he blew his nose. A werewolf standing near the front of the bus scratched himself by rubbing against a handrail pole. Across the aisle, a vampire reapplied her lipstick.

Just when the young mother thought that the old woman was going to leave them alone and mind her own business, the old witch suddenly turned toward them and cackled, as she reached out and gently pinched the baby's nose between two knuckles on her right hand.

"I've got your nose!" the old woman screeched pulling her hand away and placing her thumb between the knuckles that previously held the baby's nose.

"I've got your nose," the old woman repeated.

The baby giggled, all traces of his previous tears were gone.

"I'd appreciate it if you would not touch my baby," the young mother's voice shook.

"Oh, it's alright," the old woman ignored, "all my grandchildren are grown now."

"Well, I'm sorry to hear that, but that doesn't mean..."

"PEAK," the old woman interrupted covering her eyes beneath her palms.

The young mother sighed; the baby grinned.

The old Greyhound pulled over at another bus stop.

"...A..." the old woman leaned-in close.

The baby grabbed the old woman's nose with clawed fingers, and ripped it from her face.

A torrent of deep red blood gushed from the hole where the old woman's nose use to be.

When the shocked old woman lowered her trembling hands from her face the baby quickly bit off two of her fingers, just above the knuckles, with a set of long, sharp incisors that closely resembled the fangs of a snake.

"BOO!" said the baby as the old woman scrambled from her seat, screaming.

The baby threw the chunk of bloody nose to the floorboards like a discarded pacifier.

"He said his first word!" cried the young mother joyfully as the old woman stumbled into the aisle all the while trying to cover the blood-spouting hole in the middle of her face with gnarled hands. One of which now lacked a full set of wrinkled, age-spotted fingers.

The old woman drew the attention of the other passengers with her screaming trauma.

As the bus had arrived at their stop, the young mother and her baby assumed the form of bats, and they flew from the old Greyhound into the rain and fog.

THE END

CAT & MOUSE

Jethro Bowham celebrated the evening following the afternoon of his wife's funeral. On the way home from the burial as he passed The Heavenly Hills Cemetery he stopped at Myer's Market and picked up a T-bone steak, deli potato salad, a chocolate pie from the bakery, a twelve pack of Miller Genuine Draft, and a small bottle of tequila, the kind with a little, white, marinating worm soaking at the bottom of the bottle.

He drank two of the beers as he drove his old Chevy pickup home passing few other vehicles on the long, straight country road surrounded by corn crops, periodically singing "*Ding, Dong, The Witch Is Dead*" between making up and reciting out loud testimonial toasts and epitaphs of a similar sentiment.

It was the dog days of summer; hot: sticky, roasting and without relief.

He drove with all the windows down, radio blasting, and mind reeling with delight.

After an hour and a half driving flat mile after flat mile passing the same view of endless agriculture with every turn of the wheel, he finally arrived home. A small clapboard-style one story shack with peeling paint and half its windows cracked sitting on the final ten acres of what was once a large and thriving farm in the middle of nowhere, somewhere in rural western Iowa.

He parked the old pickup truck near the crumbling barn, grabbing the groceries from the truck's rusted flatbed where the bags had tipped over and the groceries had scattered all over the back of the truck. He gathered them happily. Nothing could bring his celebratory mood down.

On his way into the house, he stopped at the rusted metal

mail box dented with birdshot sitting atop a leaning wooden post and retrieved his mail: mostly overdue bills, sales flyers, and political ads from campaigning assholes for whom he would never vote.

His brother, Jedediah, sent a condolence card, which was very unlike his brother. Jethro was pretty sure it was his brother's wife, Mary, who had actually sent the Hallmark cardboard. The handwritten note inside contained feminine loops and curves in the penmanship. Jethro rarely heard from his brother and his wife, ever since they moved to sunny California and joined some nutty religious cult, preparing for Armageddon or some such bullshit. Jethro threw the card into the trash.

He was five beers and three tequila shots into his celebration, and feeling pretty fine attired in his favorite sweat pants and T-shirt sitting in front of the boob tube watching an old "*Charlie's Angels*" rerun while eating his dinner from a TV tray.

After he burped his way to the end of his meal, he raised a half-empty Miller bottle and slurred a final tribute: "*Burn in Hell, Brenda,*" as he leaned onto one butt cheek and let pass the gas already brewing in his belly from the just consumed deli salad.

Brenda Bowham was a bitch.

And '*was*' stood out to him as being the best word in that sentence.

She bitched and complained in the morning, and she bitched and complained in the afternoon, and she bitched and complained in the evening. Jethro would have bet what remained of the farm that she bitched and complained in her sleep, bitched and complained in her dreams.

From sun up to sun down, if she wasn't mocking him about one thing then she was criticizing him about another. She didn't like his family. She didn't like his hair. She didn't like his hobbies. She didn't like his breath. Her list of dislikes was endless. In the early days of their marriage, he tried to please her: he changed his hair, he dropped his hobbies, he ate more mints, and he even saw less of his family.

Happy wife, happy life, wasn't that what they always said?

So in the beginning he put effort into pleasing Brenda. This ended when he realized that nothing would ever please her, *could* ever please her.

Complaining was her comfort, discord her delight.

He only married her because he had knocked her up. Everyone told him it was the right thing to do, so he did. That was before he really knew anything about her. Once the shackles were firmly locked, she lost the baby. Figures. He sometimes wondered if she really ever was even pregnant or if that was just some trick to trap him. A ploy for matrimony. Either way, it worked. He married a stranger perhaps under false pretenses.

Then he got to know the real nightmare he married.

And for the next thirty-two years all she did was nag him.

She nagged him about his job. She nagged him about his drinking. She nagged him about money. She nagged him about chores. She nagged him about everything, and she nagged him about nothing. The clothes he wore, the way he spoke, his very existence: she approved of nothing, nada, none of it. And she had no trouble saying so. Every day, and in every way, she let him know she disapproved of everything about him.

In fact the only thing in this world she *did* approve of, the only thing in this world she even seemed to *like* was that damn cat of hers. A mangy stray she adopted a decade before her death.

She called him Hunter (the cat was always stalking something).

He called it Road Kill (based on the concept of 'wishful thinking').

Jethro Bowham hated that damn cat as much as he hated his dead wife. There were many reasons for his animosity toward both. The fact that his wife liked the cat more than she liked him significant among them.

"Fuckin mangy beast!" he slurred, somewhat referring to both.

And in that exact moment, he thought he heard the damn thing howl at the back door but when he went out to investigate he found nothing in the yard moving among the shadows cast by the moonlight. He returned to the recliner by way of drunken stagger.

"Nothing but a stinking pussy," he muttered, again referring to both his deceased wife and her damn cat.

As he downed the last of the tequila, as he crunched on the white worm between yellowing teeth, as he set aside the TV tray and pushed the recliner back into a lounging position, he broke out into a huge smile.

Tomorrow was Sunday and the celebration was scheduled to continue. For the first time in a long time he wasn't planning on going to church because Brenda wasn't here to nag him into attending. Other than the normal everyday chores involved in running the farm, the day was his to do as he pleased.

Jethro Bowham had but one big task planned for the day.

Tomorrow he was going to kill that damn cat.

♦ ♦ ♦ ♦ ♦ ♦ ♦ ♦ ♦ ♦ ♦ ♦

Born in the cornfields, the kitten Brenda adopted and domesticated a decade ago was the only one to survive from the feral stray who died giving birth to the litter. When Brenda went into town one day, Jethro shot the others and buried them in secret before she could take any more under her wing.

Hunter the kitten was a scraggly-haired fur ball of indeterminate breed with a matted coat of black, white, tan, grey, and yellow patches of long, tangled fur. No matter how much Brenda washed and groomed him, combed and bathed him, he remained scraggly, matted, and tangled throughout his life.

The wonky eye didn't do much to help soften his harsh appearance either. Milky, greenish, with a webbing of pink veins covering its surface, Hunter was born with a blind left eye that constantly twitched and shifted as if seeing moving objects of which his other eye, the right, was oblivious. Most disturbing of all was when the cat slept the wonky eye remained open, twitching and shifting.

Hunter's personality was as mangy as his coat. Nervous, shifty, always on edge, it was a wild cat at heart, regardless of Brenda's attention. It was the type of cat that always appeared to be up to something sneaky, always on the prowl, a hunter.

If he wasn't stalking prey in the hay loft of the barn or under the house, Hunter could be found in the rows of the cornfields sneaking up on birds and mice with the silent stealth of an unattached shadow, wandering freely like a whisper on the wind.

The emotion of hatred did not belong exclusively to Jethro. As far as Hunter the cat was concerned, the feeling was mutual. The damn thing raised its hackles and hissed at him at every encounter, before turning and running away from him, as it always did, growling in its throat.

Jethro had wanted to kill the cat even when Brenda had still been alive. He had tried to catch it on many occasions, but Hunter had always eluded him. Not once in over ten years did the cat ever come close enough for Jethro to even touch him. Hunter was *that* vigilant. He would have just shot the damn thing as he had its kitten siblings, but Brenda would have heard the gun go off if she were home and when she wasn't, well, somehow Hunter always knew when not to be seen.

He and Brenda had contentious fights over the years regarding Hunter the cat and he had lost most of them. They argued over the wasting of hard earned money (over two-hundred dollars) spent on vet bills when it came home bloody, limping, and missing half an ear from a cat fight years ago. They argued over whether or not it should be allowed into the house.

Jethro insisted that the cat remain outdoors, but Brenda brought him into the house every time his back was turned. So every night at sundown, Jethro made sure he put the cat out before going to bed. And every morning, like clockwork, he left a gift for Brenda at the back door outside on the porch.

Mice, birds, snakes, squirrels, even a beaver once.

Even with the wonky eye, Hunter was an effective hunter and over the years, he left a menagerie of dead animals on their doorstep. Brenda would fawn over every carcass that cat gave her like it was a mink coat. She would thank him and give him treats and pet him and talk to him with 'baby talk' until Jethro wanted to puke.

"Why don't you just whip a tit out and nurse him!" he once sarcastically said.

"Be better than your lips on em!" she spat back turning from him to pamper her cat with belly rubs. After the miscarriage that christened the start of their marriage, they never had any other children and, for Brenda, Hunter was their only baby.

A baby Jethro Bowham was happy he now had the opportunity to retroactively abort.

♦ ♦ ♦ ♦ ♦ ♦ ♦ ♦ ♦ ♦ ♦ ♦

He awoke on Sunday morning, the day after his wife's burial, with a bad hangover. He had fallen asleep in the recliner while watching TV and he was startled awake at 6 am by a Fire & Brimstone spouting televangelist screaming a diatribe proclaiming that Satan was going to persecute and torment anyone within the sound of his broadcast voice who didn't take a solemn vow to send the televangelist ten percent of their yearly income.

He sat up and the plate of half-eaten chocolate pie that remained cradled in his lap all night as he slept fell to the floor in a clatter, rattling his throbbing head and startling him into pained alertness. He rubbed his face, and pushed the recliner into an upright position.

He vaguely remembered dreaming of howls. Agonizing cries coming from outside the farm house, high pitched wails of despair coming from Hunter the cat, as if the mangy beast was somehow aware of, and mourning the death of his beloved mistress. The nightmare, dreamt under the influence of alcohol and remembered through the haze of a severe hangover, gave realism to the cat's howls.

Perhaps, Jethro considered, it hadn't been a dream.

He turned off the TV and farted. He rose from the recliner and farted. He coughed, stretched, and farted his way into the bathroom where he farted while he peed.

After breakfast, Jethro changed his clothes, and he retrieved his shotgun from the closet of the bedroom he had shared with his wife before the bitch bit the dust and he loaded it with a smile.

When he had his shoes on and laced up, he went to the back door with the intention of going out and looking for that damn cat before starting on the chores of the day. When he opened the door, he stopped in his tracks, frozen at the sight of what lay on the porch before him.

Hunter had left another gift.

It was a finger. A human finger.

About three inches long and severed to include the knuckle, the finger lay at his feet on the sun-faded WELCOME mat. There was a faint scrape of pink fingernail polish on the manicured nail at one end of the severed finger and the jagged, bloody mess at the other end looked like the digit had been chewed and clawed from the hand of its owner.

Jethro looked around the yard but saw no sign of the cat.

Retrieving a wad of toilet paper from the bathroom so that he could pick it up without touching it with his bare hands, Jethro brought the finger into the house and set it on the kitchen table. He sat down in one of the adjacent chairs and just stared at it.

Contemplating the strange sight cradled in the wad of toilet paper crumpled on his kitchen table, he wondered if he should call the police; call his neighbor, Carl Cressel, who lived about a mile and a half up the road; or just bury the damn thing out in the back field.

He turned the wad of tissue paper to get a look at the finger from a different angle.

It looked like a woman's finger.

It looked familiar.

He got an idea.

He rose from the chair, left the kitchen, and went into the bathroom. From the medicine cabinet he took a small bottle and returned with it to the kitchen table. He sat in the chair before the finger and shook the bottle, mixing the liquid inside. He unscrewed the bottle's cap and used the brush attached to the underside of the lid to brush a small line of Brenda's favorite nail polish onto the linoleum tabletop next to the wad of tissue paper cradling the severed finger.

"What the hell..." he muttered.

The line of polish on the table and the patch of polish on the nail of the severed finger appeared extremely similar in color and hue, perfecting into an exact match as the former dried.

Frowning in confusion, Jethro farted in contemplation.

"How the hell did Road Kill get this?" he muttered.

Staring at the strange, severed finger, Jethro couldn't help but to feel that he was looking at a small piece of his dead wife, somehow returned from the grave.

He flushed it, along with the wad of tissue down the toilet.

♦ ♦ ♦ ♦ ♦ ♦ ♦ ♦ ♦ ♦ ♦ ♦

The shotgun slung over his left shoulder, Jethro Bowham walked the rows of the cornfield that afternoon. The Indian summer heat bore down relentlessly on the flatlands of western Iowa baking the dirt, the ground, the earth into a dry and dusty crust.

He made a point of finishing his work chores (yes, even on a Sunday, even with a hangover, the farm had chores that required his attention) early, in the cool of the morning, before setting out after lunch – a half-eaten Hungry Man Salisbury steak TV dinner - on his quest to hunt down Hunter.

He was still feeling the effects of his morning hangover. His mouth was dry, his eyes stung, his stomach grumbled, his head throbbed, his energy drained, yet he moved with staunch determination and unwavering resolve. He had but one task left for the day and he intended to complete it.

Road Kill's as good as dead! He thought.

He began his search by driving the perimeter of his property, searching the rural highways running alongside his cornfields in his old Chevy pickup looking for an automobile accident that might explain how that damn cat could have gotten his claws (so to speak) on that finger. In other words, *real* road kill.

As he suspected would be the case, he found no wreaked cars, no dead women missing a digit, no female survivors searching in a daze for their missing finger on the side of the road. He knew this would be the outcome because he was pretty sure that somehow the finger Hunter the cat left on his doorstep belonged to his dead wife.

He parked the pickup truck and entered the cornfields on foot.

Up one row and down the next, he walked like his shadow, with the practiced stealth of a veteran hunter. Occasionally he called out to Hunter in a pleasant tone of voice he had never feigned before. Coldly warm, filled with false affection, and deceptively down right friendly. The *more flies with honey* approach.

Walking close to the row of corn on his right to take advantage of the meager shade provided by the tall stalks, he paused to swipe away the sweat dripping from his brow with a snot-encrusted handkerchief. Stuffing the disgusting piece of cloth into the back pocket of his filthy blue jeans, he continued his search.

Jethro had not seen Hunter the cat since the day of Brenda's death. It had been skulking around the yard near the back door that day howling just as it had last night in his dreams as Brenda was drawing her last breath. It cried that day as if it knew what was happening inside the house, as if it knew its mistress was dying.

Something moved, barely perceived from the corner of his eye.

He froze, raised the shotgun, and slowly turned.

He saw nothing unusual, no cat.

Just the wind, swaying the stalks, tricking his eye.

He continued walking.

There had been a break in the 'gifts' Road Kill left at the back door during the four days between Brenda's death and her burial. No dead birds. No chewed mice. In fact there had been no sign of the mangy beast at all during that time. Jethro thought it odd that the giving of the gifts of dead prey ceased during that period only to resume on the exact same day his wife was buried with the appearance of the severed finger.

He emerged from the corn rows. He had reached the northern edge of his property, bordered by a ranch-style fence that was warped and twisted from age and weather. He leaned the shotgun along the railing of the fence and rubbed the aching shoulder that had carried it.

Beyond the fence, across the highway, the Cressel farm spread out as far as the eye could see from left to right and straight out into the horizon. Jethro could see Carl Cressel riding his tractor about a half a mile away and he waved but Carl must not have seen him as there was no return greeting.

Jethro was using the snot-encrusted handkerchief to wipe his face again when he was startled by a rustling sound coming from behind him in the corn rows. He spun on his heals and instinctively reached for the shotgun which he only managed to knock over.

Something crawling low to the ground scurried back behind the shelter of the stalks. Fumbling and frightened, Jethro managed to pick up the shotgun, aim it in the general direction of the retreating creature, and then quickly calmed himself into having the restraint not to randomly fire into the cornfield.

Why am I so nervous?

Hesitantly, trembling slightly, Jethro stepped away from the fence and reentered the rows of the cornfield. He turned in the direction he had last seen the scuttling creature but found nothing in the area.

He passed through the stalks into the next row and a black crow suddenly fluttered from the ground up, flapping its wings against his face before flying off in an angry squeal of caws and squawks.

Startled, Jethro almost fired the shotgun in reflex.

Heart pounding, he took several deep breaths in an effort to calm his nerves. After a moment, he let out a long sigh and continued his search.

"Here kitty, kitty," Jethro called sarcastically, laughing at his feigned frivolity even as his trembling hand rattled the butt of the rifle. "Come taste a belly-full of lead."

For the rest of the afternoon, he searched the cornfields.

Hunter the cat was never seen that day.

♦ ♦ ♦ ♦ ♦ ♦ ♦ ♦ ♦ ♦ ♦ ♦

But that night, Brenda visited.

Jethro had gone to bed early, sun-burnt and sore from his time in the fields that day. Angry that the damn cat had eluded his shotgun, he lay in bed steaming from the late summer heat and the disappointment. Sleep came slowly as he lay there for hours, staring at the ceiling, before it arrived.

Brenda came to him in a dream.

Well, what was left of her came to him.

He was back in the corn rows, deep in the crop, searching for that mangy cat, when she stepped out from behind the stalks and confronted him. Bright daylight vividly revealed that she had recently returned from her grave. Her burial clothes were now shredded and muddy, her hair was tangled and matted, her face was torn and bloody.

She was rotting flesh. Her skin had shriveled and was peeling away from the gangrene-infected muscles that atrophied beneath. Both of her eyes resembled Road Kill's wonky eye; milky cataracts covering a dead stare. She smiled and a long, brown earthworm slid out of her mouth through cracked, bleeding lips.

"Can you feed my cat?" the corpse of his wife asked and when she raised her hand to gesture for the mangy beast to come to her, Jethro could see that she was missing one of her fingers, a bloody stump pointed at him in its place.

At that moment, a wailing howl pierced the nightmare and he sat up in bed, awakening into darkness. The only light he could see was a small red glow coming from the digital clock on his nightstand which revealed the time to be 2:37am.

Another howl confirmed the first was not part of the dream and Jethro fumbled to throw back the blankets and climb out of bed. Grabbing the shotgun leaning against the bedpost and a flashlight from the nightstand, he ran down the hall through the kitchen and to the back door. He switched on the porch light and the shade covering the window in the door lit up in the yellow glow of the light beyond the glass.

With his heart pounding and his hand trembling, he hesitated with his fingers on the doorknob. Another piercing howl startled his nerves and he quickly removed his hand from the knob and stepped back from the door.

Road Kill sounded angry, vengeful, and rabid.

The next howl devolved into a guttural growl.

Taking a deep breath Jethro reached out, clutched the knob, and flung open the back door. Standing in the doorframe, looking out into the yard, he raised the flashlight and the shotgun simultaneously.

The crisp night air carried the chirps and clicks of a multitude of crickets and other nocturnal insects. A full moon revealed a clear night sky, yet a fine white mist clung close to the ground and it rolled like waves on an ocean tide in a light breeze that swayed the corn stalks in the shimmer of starlight.

He saw no sign of the mangy beast in the yard, but he nearly jumped out of his skin when another piercing howl shrieked into momentary silence the cacophonous song of the cicada.

As the feline's screams and cries faded and the chirping

sound of the crickets returned, the reverberating echo revealed the direction of the sound of the cat's howls to be coming from the rows of the cornfield.

Jethro aimed the shotgun in the direction he thought the cat was hiding, but he did not open fire. He stared intently into the mist surrounding the base of the stalks in the row closest to the house watching for the kind of movement that indicated the presence of a small animal, but no movement caught his eye's attention.

He realized in that moment that the cat's cries he had heard and attributed to his dreams the night before were probably real. Road Kill had begun wailing the night his mistress was buried.

Jethro stood in the doorway for several more minutes, listening to the howls, watching for movement in the dark. After a few moments, the cat's cries grew distant and faded, retreating deep into the rows of the cornfield until nothing rang out in his ear but the sound of the crickets. Lowering the flashlight and shotgun, retreating into the house, Jethro closed the back door and turned off the porch light.

He went back to bed, but he lay awake staring at the ceiling until dawn.

Afraid to sleep, afraid to dream.

♦ ♦ ♦ ♦ ♦ ♦ ♦ ♦ ♦ ♦ ♦ ♦

Left to run wild until dawn, his imagination provided as many terrors as any nightmare could invoke. Once he fixated on the horrific possibilities that could be awaiting him on the back porch come the morning, left as 'gifts' from his nemesis cat. His mind conjured images as terrifying as any horror movie.

He rose from the bed as the first rays of sunlight cut through the part in the curtains covering the bedroom window. He yawned. He farted. He dressed in the clothes he had worn the day before found crumpled on the floor at the foot of the bed.

When he left the bedroom, he took the shotgun with him.

At first he avoided the kitchen altogether. But hunger finally forced him to the refrigerator where he devoured whatever the brown rice thing was in the orange Tupperware container while standing over the sink. As he ate, he avoided even looking at the back door.

Finally, his belly full, his attention alert, his nerves steady, he picked up the shotgun leaning against the stove and he turned to face the back door.

If there was a 'gift' to receive it could not be avoided forever.

The walk across the kitchen floor took some of the resolve from his legs and he felt a little shaky as he stopped and stood at the threshold. Reaching out with a hand that struggled to remain steady, he gripped the doorknob and slowly turned it.

When he opened the door the first thing he noticed was how the mist of the night had risen by morning into a full blown fog bank, covering the corn rows behind an opaque curtain of roiling white billows, an indication that fall was finally coming.

Jethro lowered his gaze to the boards of the porch beyond the doorstep.

Looking up from the WELCOME mat at his feet, in a small puddle of bloody viscera, a single human eyeball, attached in the back to a tangle of shredded nerve endings and torn muscles, cast an unwavering and accusatory dead gaze at him. He recognized the look of that cold glare. As he stared down on it he realized it had stared him down on many occasions. It belonged to his dead wife. The pupil and iris matched her same shade of Bitch Brown.

"What the f..."

A black crow landed on the outer step of the porch, cawed and took a couple of hop-steps toward the bloody orb. Jethro clapped his hands and shooed it away.

He scanned the yard but saw no sign of Hunter the cat, just other crows gathering, and his attention was drawn back to the grotesque little ball at his feet. There was no doubt in his mind that this was yet another piece of his dead wife returned home from her grave.

"How can this be?" he muttered.

First the finger and now the eye, it made no sense. Even if Road Kill knew where it was there was no way the mangy beast could make the long journey to his mistress's grave and back each night.

Let alone, dig her up.

And bring back the pieces.

"Well that settles it," he declared. It was time to get to the bottom of all this once and for all. It was time to find out how that damn cat was performing this mischief. It was time to put a stop to this nightmare. It was time to do something he thought he would never do.

It was time to visit his wife's grave.

He kicked the bloody eyeball off the WELCOME mat, and it rolled off the porch into the dirt of the yard. It wasn't long before a small murder of crows was fighting over the tender morsel.

Jethro closed the door on the avian battle and retreated into the house.

♦ ♦ ♦ ♦ ♦ ♦ ♦ ♦ ♦ ♦ ♦ ♦

That afternoon, he set out in the Chevy pickup for the long drive east.

Once again he drove with all of the windows down, radio blasting, and mind reeling.

The dog days of summer still lingered; hot, sticky, roasting, without relief.

After an hour and a half, driving flat mile after flat mile, passing the same view of endless agriculture with every turn of the wheel, he approached his destination.

About four miles past Myer's Market and The Heavenly Hills Cemetery, he turned the Chevy pick-up down an unmarked, gravel road and continued into the woods for another four miles. At several points, the gravel road disappeared into the overgrowth of wilderness and Jethro was thankful for the truck's four-wheel drive.

Far from civilization, deep in the rural wilderness of western Iowa, the terrain eventually turned too rough for the Chevy, so he parked the pickup and climbed out of the truck. He stood for a moment and silently debated whether or not he should bring the shovel he had placed in the flatbed and decided he could always come back for it if he needed it.

Taking a deep breath, he set off on foot deeper into the woods.

He walked for over an hour before he came to the spot where three days prior he had buried her. At a small clearing, beneath the dried husk of a dead and leaning tree, a small patch of earth appeared recently dug, churned, and repacked.

The shallow grave he had buried her in remained as he had left it: unknown, unmarked, and undisturbed. He stared at it in confusion. The drive had taken long enough to give him the time to convince himself that somehow Road Kill was actually making the same journey, night after night, and returning with little bits of his dead spouse.

He had come to expect an exposed hole in the ground where the mangy beast would have extracted the 'gifts' he bestowed. He expected to see a half unburied corpse, missing a finger and an eye, pulled from the cold ground.

He sat down on a log and contemplated the undisturbed grave.

The whole confusing thing began on the Wednesday before he buried her.

After nagging him into attending Bible Study with her at the church that evening, Brenda had come to him with the announcement that she was leaving him. He greeted this as great news until she also announced that she intended to force him into selling the farm and then she planned to hire a lawyer to help her screw him out of every cent she could get from him.

This led to a verbal argument,which led to a physical

fight. He had gotten some really good punches in but then, so did she. In no time, they were both bloody and bruised.

The fight ended when Jethro picked up the shotgun.

For four days he sat on the bedroom floor, in a pool of her blood, still wearing his Sunday finest, getting drunk on tequila, and staring at her dead body.

Finally, on the following Saturday, he arose from his bedroom floor (no small feat as the dried blood created a strong adhesive to his skin and clothes) just after sundown and he gathered her body onto the flatbed of the Chevy.

He buried her at this spot by moonlight with a night owl bearing sole witness.

He made the mistake of telling his brother, Jedediah, during a rare telephone call (Jethro still didn't know what compelled him to answer it) during one of the hazy days staring at her body in the bedroom that she had passed away following a short illness. After hanging up, he realized that from now on it would be best, if anyone should ask, to say that she had gone to visit her sister somewhere far off and that the date of her return was unknown.

He sat for over an hour, staring at the patch of earth where he had interred his nagging wife, just as he had on the night he buried her with so many questions swirling around his confused head.

Eventually he walked away from his wife's grave and he returned to the Chevy pick-up with a million unanswered questions running through his mind and uncertainty in his heart.

But one thing was for sure…

Even if he had to fire bomb all ten acres of his farm, that fucking cat was a dead fucking cat!

♦ ♦ ♦ ♦ ♦ ♦ ♦ ♦ ♦ ♦ ♦ ♦

He drove back home in silence; windows up, radio off, mind numb.

His foot heavy on the gas pedal, he made the return trip in under an hour.

When he parked the Chevy pickup near the barn, he sprinted into the house and remained inside just long enough to retrieve the shotgun and then he was back outside crossing the yard entering the cornfield.

He did not move between the rows of corn stalks with the silent stealth of an experienced hunter. He marched through the field with a seething anger and determination that precluded patient pursuit.

"GET OUT HERE, YOU MANGY SHIT!" he bellowed.

He covered all ten acres of what was left of his farm twice before exhaustion calmed his anger, and still that damn cat was nowhere to be found. He was walking back to the house when the solution came to him...

If Road Kill hunts by moonlight, then so would he.

♦ ♦ ♦ ♦ ♦ ♦ ♦ ♦ ♦ ♦ ♦ ♦

He waited until midnight.

Then he decided to wait a little longer. An hour later, he thought he heard a howl. It came from outside at the back of the house near the kitchen. He rose from the recliner, grabbed the shotgun, rushed through the kitchen, and peeked past the shade hanging in the window of the back door.

The night mist had returned to the cornfields and a full moon revealed Hunter the cat crossing the yard sneaking into the rows of the corn stalks. He released another feline cry into the frosty air before disappearing behind the crops.

Quietly, Jethro opened the door and exited the house. No gift had yet to be bestowed upon the WELCOME mat and he looked around the yard. The crisp, cold air did not cut through his determination. He felt nothing but exhilaration as he silently crossed the yard following the same path as Road Kill.

He aimed the shotgun on the ground ahead of him as he

walked, as he had left behind the flashlight in favor of stealth. Only the moonlight guided his way shining bright in a night sky sprinkled with an abundance of sparkling stars.

He entered the corn rows where the cat had entered, the moonlight instantly diminishing in the surrounding shadows of the tall stalks. He could not see his prey, but he could still hear it.

The mangy beast's howls were escalating. He followed the sound row by row deeper into the cornfield, stalking his prey. It never occurred to him that it was the other way around, that he was being led into danger, that *he* was the one being stalked.

Road Kill howled again, sounding further away, and Jethro picked up his pace.

Hurrying to catch up, he lost track of his position within the crops.

When he pushed his way between the stalks into the next row, he was startled to come face to face with an entity standing before him possessing an impossibly distorted physique and glowing yellow eyes.

Its legs were crooked and bent at wrong angles, and yet it stood nearly eight feet tall in the torn and ragged clothes of a derelict with outstretched arms that reached further than humanly possible. Its bulbous head leaned to one side under the weight of an asymmetrical cranium and the rictus grin stretched over what vaguely appeared to be a human-like face sneered like a demon escaped from the depths of Hell.

Shuffling backward, away from the crooked giant, he stumbled over his own feet, landed on his butt, and bit his tongue. He dropped the shotgun but quickly retrieved it.

He nearly shot the twisted figure standing in front of him before he realized it was only the harmless scarecrow he had erected on a wooden post years ago to stand guard at the center of his crop and frighten off the scavenger birds that ate into his profits.

The disturbing grin had been drawn on and the glowing eyes were bike reflectors recasting the light from the full moon. Its clothes were once his own.

Jethro almost laughed out loud but in that moment another impossible figure stepped out from behind the scarecrow and shock threw him into paralysis.

The corpse of his dead wife stood before him.

She still wore the church clothes he had buried her in, the same ones she had been wearing when they fought, when he had killed her. They were now shredded, bloody, and mud stained; a large shotgun hole in the center of her blouse revealed shattered ribs.

She was missing a finger.

She was missing an eye.

She smiled and just as it had in his nightmare, a long earthworm slid out from between her rotting lips. She looked at him with both a bloody, hollow hole and a filmy dark eye that still somehow conveyed all of the distain and contempt she had felt for her husband while still alive.

Jethro, still sitting in the dirt, tried to raise the shotgun but there was no strength in his arms. He wanted to get up and run but he was held still by a mind-numbing terror.

Brenda's corpse raised her hand and pointed the stump where her missing finger belonged and she smiled at him, revealing chipped and rotting teeth.

"Can you feed my cat?" she purred.

Suddenly, with a piercing howl, an incandescent set of eyes opened up near Brenda's bare, black feet and suddenly Hunter the cat stood beside her gangrene corpse.

His paralysis broke just enough for Jethro to let out a frightened shriek.

The sound of distress awakened a multitude of glowing eyes in the mist of the cornfields around him and a ghostly pack of feral creatures stepped out from behind the stalks to surround Jethro with their howling growls.

In moments, dozens of cats surrounded him.

Hunter the cat jumped up into his mistress's arms and licked the open wound at her eye socket lovingly, purred loudly, before jumping down and joining the other cats in the feast.

There were now over a hundred cats in the cornfield.

Brenda's corpse turned and retreated into the rows, into the mist.

The demonic cats tore at Jethro with jagged teeth and sharp claws, an army of frenzied felines. They overtook him and covered him in the bites of many fangs, the slashes of many claws. He was eaten alive, and he died screaming.

Screaming and farting.

♦ ♦ ♦ ♦ ♦ ♦ ♦ ♦ ♦ ♦ ♦ ♦

Dawn came to rural western Iowa in the glow of a golden sunrise, igniting the cornfields in a fiery blaze of amber shades and shimmering colors provoking the Cressel Farm's rooster into its morning call. Shadows stretched and elongated across the dusty farm lands as the sun rose higher and a light breeze stirred the corn stalks.

On the back porch of the house belonging to Jethro and Brenda Bowham, the resident feline left a final 'gift' on the WELCOME mat near the back door, far too gruesome to describe. Bloody and chewed ragged, the sizeable chunk of flesh found there was the only piece of Jethro Bowham ever to be found. His wife, Brenda Bowham remains missing to this day. In their absence, before it was discovered they were missing, the farm became overrun with stray, feral cats.

A Hunter among them.

MEOW

(THE END)

SECRET SANTA

Carol Singer could have taken the five cans of Purr-fect Vittles cat food through one of the self-checkout registers, but she always became intimidated and confused by the price scanners one was required to figure out on their own. Instead she opted to wait behind a large family with an overflowing shopping cart of groceries at check-out stand four.

With her perpetual smile and ever present good cheer, Carol set the stack of cans on the back of the register's conveyor belt, using a plastic divider to separate her items from the food of the family of abundant resources, as they continued to place more and more groceries onto the belt from the unending depths of their shopping cart.

Carol dug through her purse for the needed coupon, found the tattered slip of paper, torn from a newspaper discarded in a neighbor's trash can, and she placed it under the small tower of feline food.

"That'll be three hundred and seventeen dollars and sixty-four cents," Eve, one of Carol's favorite cashiers informed the family, and soon the well fed bunch was carrying their bags out of the store in outstretched armloads.

"Hi, Carol, it's good to see you again, how have ya been, hon?" Eve asked as Carol stepped up to the register.

"I'm doing well. Happy holidays," Carol replied. "Are you enjoying the season?"

Eve gave her a strange look.

"The holidays were great," the cashier recalled, "but it's nice to get back to normal again. Did you get yourself another cat, Hon? You've picked up a lot of cat food lately; you're not taking in more animals are you?"

"No, it's still just me, Snowball, and Lumpacoal," Carol smiled.

"Lumpacoal? That's an unusual name," Eve replied.

"It's from the Christmas poem about how the naughty children get a lump of coal in their Christmas stockings from Santa when they misbehave. 'Lumpacoal', get it? He's a solid black cat and my little girl, Snowball, is all white," Carol explained.

"Cute," Eve replied, placing the cans into a plastic bag. "With the coupon it comes to a total of two dollars and fifty-four cents."

Carol dug into her purse for the cash. She had pre-counted it out at home and she knew before leaving her apartment that she had just enough, with the coupon, for the purchase.

"Of course, now that the holidays are over, they're cutting everybody's hours around here now..." Eve lamented.

Carol retrieved a single dollar bill and five quarters from the main compartment of the purse. She did not immediately see the remainder of the cash within the tattered, old handbag, so she began digging around inside the imitation leather pouch.

"...which is really going to hurt now that we're sending two of our kids through college..." Eve continued.

Carol found another dime and a nickel, only fourteen cents to go.

People were starting to get in line behind her.

She was sure she had the money, but she was getting nervous.

Another nickel and two more pennies were found.

"...of course, the union is supposed to guarantee us so many hours, but you know how that usually goes..." Eve rambled.

Where ***are*** *those coins?* Carol wondered, beginning to panic, desperately digging through the purse.

Someone in line behind her gave an impatient sigh, and Carol's nerves responded by increasing the tremor in her searching fingers. She dropped two of the pennies she had already palmed back into the purse.

"...and it'll get crazy around here again when Easter comes, particularly in the florist department..." Eve complained.

Carol located the last of the coins needed to complete the transaction, and she handed over the cash with shaky hands. She was even perspiring a little bit.

That was close, she thought; closing the purse without a penny to spare.

"There you go, Hon," Eve said, handing her the receipt. "You take care of yourself now, ya hear?"

"Thank you, Eve. Merry Christmas," Carol replied, taking the receipt and the bag of canned cat food, unaware of the strange look the cashier again expressed at the reference to the yuletide holiday, as Carol stepped away from the counter and exited the store.

She walked past the bus stop she usually took when going to the store as she did not have the fifty cents required to ride, and she began the long walk home. A path that led her tired feet through three miles of inner city danger.

Carol passed a group of kids playing near, and ignoring, a car on fire in the street. She cut through a dirt field, covered in shattered glass, crushed aluminum cans, and discarded hypodermic needles, where a group of homeless men huddled around a barrel fire, and a bottle of whisky.

She was followed for three blocks by a stray pack of desperately thin, scraggly, scrawny dogs, who only lost interest in her after they spotted a younger woman carrying a baby while holding the hand of a little girl, dressed in a red parka, and the slathering, eagerly growling pack abandoned her to pursue the young mother and her children.

When she arrived at the rundown urban housing complex she called home, it was dusk. She was putting the key into the peeling paint, front door of her fifth-floor apartment, unit 522, when a woman's voice startled her as it called out softly from somewhere behind her.

"Ms. Singer? May I have a moment?"

Carol turned and saw a pretty, young woman, perhaps in her mid-thirties, holding a briefcase-like handbag, and a manila file folder, as she walked briskly toward her down the long stretch of the common-community hallway, directly toward her.

"My name is Ivy Garland. I'm with the city's Department of Social Services, Ms. Singer, and I've been asked to stop by for a quick check up to see how you're doing today. Do you have a few minutes for some questions?"

"I'm always hospitable for company at the holidays," Carol replied, struggling with her key in the doorknob's lock. "Let me just get this door open so we can chat comfortably inside."

After a moment she opened the door to her apartment, stepped inside the dark dwelling, flicked a wall switch to illuminate a lamp on a table by the door, then she turned to her guest.

"Come on in and have a seat, I'm just getting back from the store, so if you'll give me a moment to set this bag in the kitchen, I'll just be a moment," Carol said motioning toward the couch as she stepped into an adjacent room.

Ivy, the social worker, stepped into a dingy apartment, sparse of furniture. There was a couch, an end table with a lamp, a chair, and a coffee table. An old, obsolete model of a home computer sat dark on a folding card table in the far corner with an old white cat sleeping on the keyboard.

The gloom of obvious poverty was offset by an overly festive display of Christmas decorations that adorned every surface, wall, and corner of the room. There was a village of ceramic gingerbread cottages arranged on the cotton-snow covered coffee table, populated by miniature plastic Christmas revelers and, flanking a bent and tarnished artificial Christmas tree with metallic limbs and bristles, a couple of three foot tall, mechanical mannequins of Santa and Mrs. Claus, which squeaked as they nodded their heads and raised and lowered the candy canes in their hands.

"Would you like a cup of coffee, or water, or something?" Carol called from the kitchen.

"No, thank you," replied Ivy, the social worker, taking a seat on the sofa while also taking note of its worn-out upholstery covered in pet fur. "This will only take a few minutes."

"So, what's this all about, Miss Garland?" Carol asked, returning from the kitchen, having removed the sweater she wore on her errand out, revealing a blouse embroidered with decorative holly and berry trim suggesting yuletide cheer.

"Please call me Ivy, there's nothing formal in my visit here today," Ivy, the social worker, replied setting her purse on the floor near her feet, as she opened the manila file-folder. "I must say, it's not often you get to enjoy Christmas decorations in March. If you don't mind my asking, have you become physically unable to take them down and pack them away, since putting them up for the holidays?"

"No, no, not at all," Carol replied with a smile, taking a seat on the opposite end of the couch. "I always do it this way, I just love the holidays! Christmas is my favorite. Every year I always leave Christmas up until it's time to decorate for Easter. Then *that* stays up until it's time to put out the summer stuff. Before you know it, I'm ready for Halloween, and then Thanksgiving and Christmas start all over again."

"Nothing for Valentine's Day?" Ivy, the social worker, offhandedly asked, immediately wishing she had not, as she had done so without much thought.

Carol Singer's perpetual smile slipped, her eyes suddenly seemed to focus on something beyond that moment, past the room in which they sat. An awkward silence hung in the air between the two women. Then, just as suddenly, the lapse in the ever-present good cheer passed, and the perpetual smile returned, but it now looked forced and deliberate.

"No, nothing for Valentine's Day," she replied quietly.

"So, the reason I've come here," said Ivy, the social worker, quickly changing the subject, hiding the embarrassment in her eyes by focusing them on the pages within the manila file-folder. "We received a call from a concerned neighbor who reported seeing you rummaging through her garbage cans and she was concerned for your well-being. Our office sent me out here today to make sure you are getting enough to eat and are able to take care of yourself. It's just the standard wellness check visit."

"Well, I must admit," Carol began, blushing, "that recently some *minor* financial issues have caused me to find ways of cutting back and after I stopped getting my newspaper, I started taking my neighbor's old ones out of the trash. Just for the coupons, mind you. I clip coupons, and I save a lot at the grocery store with my coupons. But I would be mortified if anyone thought I was rummaging around in their garbage for *food*! Heavens no! Is that what they told you?"

"Well, no," Ivy, the social worker, replied. "No one is trying to insult you, people are just concerned. Do you mind if I ask you a few questions?"

"I suppose that would be okay," Carol replied, struggling to retain the perpetual smile.

"It says here that you are seventy-two years old, and that you live alone, is that correct?" Ivy, the social worker, asked.

"GET OUT!" Carol snapped.

Ivy Garland looked up, startled.

"Oh, no, not you!" Carol blushed, as she pointed to the black cat sticking his head into the briefcase-like purse on the floor, at the social worker's feet. "Lumpacoal must smell something in your purse that he wants. GET OUT, LUMPACOAL! I apologize for my cat's manners; they tend to do what they want around here."

The social worker looked down and discovered a black house cat sticking half in and half out of her purse. Its head buried up to its shoulders in her bag.

"Shoo," Carol gently suggested.

The cat continued to dig around in the purse.

"I'm sure he's alright, there's nothing in there that can hurt him," Ivy, the social worker, replied. "Cats are so smart, I have one of my own; 'Whiskers', a tabby. Did you see that story on the news last night about the cat that somehow dialed and called 911 and saved his owner's life, a man who was having a heart attack? It's just amazing all the things animals know, and all the things that they can do. They really are amazing little creatures, and so much smarter than we give them credit for."

"I couldn't agree more," Carol responded, "my two cats here definitely run *this* household."

"So, do I have this information correct?" Ivy, the social worker, asked, turning her attention away from the cat rummaging through her purse, back toward the manila file-folder.

"Yes," Carol confirmed, "I'm seventy-two years old, I retired six years ago from teaching grade school, but I do not live here alone. Lumpacoal here, the male cat trying to get into your purse, and Snowball, the female cat taking a nap over there on the computer table, live here with me and, although I live on a strict monthly budget, I can assure you that I do not eat from trash cans."

"Again, no one is trying to insult you," Ivy, the social worker, informed. "Do you have other people that you see? It's not good to be isolated. Do you spend much time keeping in touch with other people on that computer?"

"I had a niece come visit me once, almost a decade ago, and while she was here she set up that computer. She promised we would keep in touch through it, but I never once heard from her, after her visit was over. It's hooked up, but I never use it."

"Do you have access to an adequate amount of food?" Ivy, the social worker, asked.

"I was just getting back from the store when you arrived," Carol smiled.

The black cat named Lumpacoal backed out of the purse with something thin and plastic held between his fanged teeth, and he disappeared into another room, unobserved, as the white cat named Snowball, yawning and stretching on the computer's keyboard, continued to purr in her sleep.

"In fact, I was just going to offer *you* something to eat," Carol continued.

"No, thank you," Ivy, the social worker, replied, closing the manila file-folder, "I think I've seen enough here to be able to report that all is fine. I'm sorry if my visit was inconvenient or uncomfortable. The Department of Social Services makes these visits out of concern for our citizens, and a desire to help humanity. If you ever do find yourself in a situation of need or despair, we hope that you'll reach out for help."

Ivy, the social worker, gathered her purse from the floor, secluded the manila file-folder within it, and she stood, extending her outstretched hand toward Carol.

"It was very nice to meet you, Ms. Singer." Ivy, the social worker, said.

"Thank you for stopping by," Carol replied, shaking the social worker's hand.

She walked Ivy Garland to the door, opened it, and she watched as the social worker walked briskly along the common community hallway away from her.

When Carol closed the door and turned away from it, she sighed.

Snowball, lying on the computer keyboard, opened her eyes, raised her head, and yawned as Lumpacoal returned to the room, no longer carrying the item he took from the briefcase-like purse moments earlier. Lumpacoal rubbed up against Carol's leg, as Snowball stood and stretched in her usual back-arching, post-nap ritual.

"I know! I know!" Carol exclaimed, good-naturedly. "You guys are hungry, you want your dinner. Let's go eat."

Snowball and Lumpacoal followed Carol into the kitchen as surely and as swiftly as the mice that followed the Pied Piper over the cliffs into the sea.

Carol took one of the cans of Purr-fect Vittles cat food from the plastic bag, and she pulled back the aluminum lid revealing a container of fatty chicken chunks and bits floating in coagulated brown gravy. She emptied the contents of the can onto two saucers, and she placed one of them on the yellowing linoleum floor.

Snowball and Lumpacoal attacked the small plate of food like there was no tomorrow; each trying to crowd the other out as they jockeyed for position around the saucer, their little furry faces pushing against each other in attempts to dominate the plate.

Carol retrieved a fork from a drawer and a napkin from a cabinet, and she took the other plate of Purr-fect Vittles cat food to the small folding table that served as her kitchen table, and she took a seat on one of the adjacent metal-framed chairs.

"You've been very sweet, having a little less than you normally do to eat, and sharing your food like this," she said, as her cats ignored her in their intent of feeding.

"Bon Appetite!" she wished them, as the perpetual smile faded with the ever-present good cheer.

Then, in silence, the three of them ate the one can of cat food that would serve as dinner for all. The cats finished quickly, Carol took some time forcing it down; by the time she was putting the plates in the sink, Snowball and Lumpacoal had disappeared into another room.

They watched a little television together in the front room – 'Wheel of Fortune' and 'Jeopardy' – with Snowball in her lap and Lumpacoal at her feet. Her eyes started getting heavy during "The Bachelor", and she drifted off for a while during 'Survivor'.

When Carol finally turned off the television, said 'goodnight' to the cats, and went into her bedroom, it was well after 11 pm.

Snowball and Lumpacoal waited until midnight to discuss the situation openly.

"Did you get it?" meowed Snowball.

"You bet," purred Lumpacoal, "easy as tuna."

"Well, bring it over to me. I'll start up the computer," mewed Snowball.

Lumpacoal left the room, as Snowball climbed up onto the folding card table and pushed a paw against the computer's power button. A few moments later, he returned with a credit card between his fanged teeth, as she brushed the pads of her paws against the computer's keyboard.

"Read me the numbers," purred Snowball, and Lumpacoal complied.

"We better order a lot before that lady realizes what happened with her credit card and comes back looking for it," Lumpacoal suggested.

"Don't worry," replied Snowball, "I've been filling up shopping carts for days now just waiting for a way to pay for it all."

"Carol deserves this," Lumpacoal reasoned.

"Of course she does," Snowball agreed, "she has a big heart."

She completed a series of transactions while he watched.

"When she had to start eating our food," Lumpacoal recalled, "I knew we had to do something. Have you noticed how thin she's getting?"

"It isn't right," Snowball opined, hitting the final BUY button on the final website shopping cart, "there should be a big Easter feast in her honor. She has a big heart. She deserves all that we're doing for her."

"She has a big heart, alright," Lumpacoal repeated in agreement, retreating with the credit card embossed with the name of the social worker, Ivy Garland, along its plastic bottom edge, as Snowball closed down the old and nearly obsolete computer and climbed down from the card table.

When Lumpacoal returned to Snowball's side, they sniffed each other's butts.

"Good job," purred Snowball.

"You too," meowed Lumpacoal.

In the morning, Carol was awakened by the doorbell.

"Just a moment," she muttered, climbing out of bed fully aware that someone standing at her front door would not be able to hear her muttering in her bedroom.

She grabbed a robe from a hook on the back of her bedroom door, and she put it on as she crossed the front room to the door.

The cats, she noticed, were nowhere to be seen.

Probably waiting in the kitchen to be fed!

She looked through the peep-hole at a young man in a polyester uniform.

"Who is it?" Carol asked, through the door.

"Delivery," the young man informed, in a loud voice.

"I didn't order anything," Carol replied, not opening the door.

"Are you Carol Singer?" the young delivery man asked.

"Yes," Carol answered, her confusion growing.

"Well, I have an order of Eggs Benedict, country bacon, English scones, assorted berries and melon wedges, and a carafe of Brazilian Gold Roast coffee for someone named Carol Singer, from her 'Secret Santa'," informed the young delivery man. "It's all paid for, do you accept delivery?"

Carol closed the bathrobe tight around her throat, and opened the door.

"My Secret Santa?" she asked, her perpetual smile now beaming bright. "Do you know who it's *really* from?"

"I'm just the delivery guy, lady. Even if it wasn't anonymous, I wouldn't know anything," the young man said, handing over the steaming bags, cartons, and containers of food.

"Thank you," Carol replied, taking the packages giving off a delicious aroma.

Unable to give a tip, she thanked him again before closing the door. Retreating into the kitchen with the unexpected breakfast, she found Snowball and Lumpacoal patiently waiting by their empty food bowl.

"Good news! You guys don't have to share your food with me this morning!" she said, as she opened a can of Purr-fect Vittles cat food, and emptied the entire contents of the container onto a single, small saucer, and placed it on the floor.

Snowball and Lumpacoal went into a feeding frenzy of ecstatic eating.

Carol Singer did the same with her unexpected breakfast.

She was just clearing away the dishes when, once again, the doorbell rang.

"Just a moment," she called out; confidant that this time

she was probably heard.

A moment later, when she opened the door, another delivery man – a much older, Asian gentlemen - stood at her threshold, holding boxes and bags that smelled of Chinese food: shrimp fried rice, chicken chow mien, egg fu young, won ton soup, and pot stickers.

"Already paid for," the Asian gentleman informed. "Secret Santa, just sign for delivery."

A few moments later, after failing to discover who was *really* behind the much appreciated gifts of food, she thanked the elderly Asian gentleman, apologized for lacking the ability to offer a monetary tip while expressing genuine gratitude. She closed the door with armfuls of aromatic boxes and bags.

Later that afternoon, while watching The Price is Right, Carol ate the lunch created by General Tso's Kitchen, as provided by an unknown benefactor whose true identity now consumed most of her fantasies.

Snowball and Lumpacoal just stared at her in that way in which cats do.

After devouring the calorie-rich meal, Carol's eyes became heavy during the Final Showcase, and she was asleep on the couch by the time The Price is Right turned into Let's Make a Deal.

The doorbell awakened her in the late afternoon, just before suppertime.

When she opened the door, she was not surprised to discover a smiling delivery man with containers of steaming, delicious smelling food.

Texas Barbeque: ribs, wings, burgers, steaks, and shrimp shish kabobs.

Corn on the cob, coleslaw, potato salad.

Even paper napkins, plastic forks, and spoons.

No charge. Secret Santa. Sorry, I don't know who it really is.

Don't worry about a tip, lady, just enjoy the barbeque!

At dinner, the cats once again enjoyed a full can of Purr-fect Vittles.

Day after day over the next week the food just kept arriving.

Monday: a fiesta of tacos, burritos, enchiladas, and quesadillas.

Tuesday: a Greek feast of Kalamata olives, feta cheeses, pitas, and gyros.

Wednesday: French cuisine; Beluga caviar and escargot, with fresh baguette.

Thursday: an Abbondanza of spaghetti and meatballs, ravioli and pizza.

Friday: fish; salmon and cod. Battered and fried. Buttered and grilled.

Saturday: steaks and potatoes, soups and salads, cakes and pies.

Sunday: a potluck of casseroles and croissants, roasts and stews.

And on the following Monday more delectable delights arrived courtesy of her Secret Santa.

Pepperidge Farms sent a crop of candied fruits and dried vegetables. Cracker Barrel sent barrels of crackers and assorted meats and cheeses. Little Debbie provided enough pastries and snack cakes to open a bakery.

The Fruit of the Month Club sent peaches, plums, and pears.

The Nut of the Month Club sent pecans and pistachios; unshelled and salted.

The Meat of the Month Club sent pepperoni and prosciutto, smoked and cured.

The Cheese of the Month Club sent parmesan and provolone, aged and cultured.

Day after day, meal after meal, around the clock, for weeks on end a feast of foods arrived at her doorstep.

All courtesy of her Secret Santa.

On the Saturday afternoon before Easter Sunday, Carol Singer stepped off her electronic weight scale with a frowning look of worried concern suppressing her perpetual smile, and stressing her ever-present good cheer.

So, I'll have to go on a diet soon, so what!

She stepped out of the bathroom, entered the front room, and announced: "Well, Snowball! Well, Lumpacoal! The time has come to take down and pack away the Christmas decorations and put up Easter! Spring is here!"

The two house cats, who lately hadn't had to share a can of Purr-fect Vittles with *each other*, let alone Carol watched indifferently as she went to work.

She retrieved the plastic storage containers from the back of the hall closet. She wrapped the ceramic Christmas village cottages in packing paper. She placed the miniature Christmas village revelers in boxes. She rolled up the sheet of cotton snow that covered the coffee table town square.

She paused for lunch when her Secret Santa sent gourmet goodies.

She removed a string of colored lights and a sash of ivy garland from the tree. She folded the Christmas tree as if she were closing an umbrella. She unplugged the squeaking Santa and Mrs. Claus mechanical mannequins.

She paused for dinner when her Secret Santa sent mouth-watering morsels.

She packed away the plastic storage containers of Christmas decorations. She brought out the plastic storage containers of Easter decorations. She set up a ceramic Easter village, complete with dapper and bonneted revelers. She plugged in a squeaking Easter Bunny mechanical mannequin. She struggled to stash away the empty plastic Easter decorations containers.

She clutched her heart and fell to the floor.

She gasped for air and closed her eyes.

Snowball and Lumpacoal approached and watched.

She stopped moving and became still.

Lumpacoal made the first move; hesitantly, he approached her.

He came in close to her face and he sniffed the air near her nose for breath.

He licked her left cheek and eyelid and received no reaction.

Snowball approached. She sniffed. She licked. She frowned.

"She has a big heart," Lumpacoal reminded, biting into Carol's left eyelid, tearing it away from her face. "I knew it would give out on her eventually."

"This was a great idea you had," Snowball admitted, beginning to chew on the prone woman's lower lip with sharp, fanged teeth. "She really deserves this."

Having removed, chewed and swallowed Carol's left eyelid, Lumpacoal began to devour the eyeball beneath the gory exposure. "It just wasn't right! When she started eating our food and feeding us less, I knew we had to do something about it," he replied.

"Did you notice how thin she was getting? It was smart to put a little meat on her bones before the big Easter feast in her honor," Snowball mewed, biting into her tongue.

"She deserves all that we are doing," Lumpacoal meowed, chewing her left eye.

The two house cats continued to eat Carol Singer's face late into the evening, moving to the softness of her belly and torso at the dawn of morning on Easter Sunday.

"She has a big heart," Snowball purred, pausing to lick the blood off her face, "when we eat our way down to it, I call dibs!"

MEOW

THE CREATURES OF DRIFTWOOD BEACH

EDITOR'S NOTE

THE FOLLOWING DOCUMENT IS A TRANSCRIPT TAKEN VERBATIM FROM A RESTORED MANUSCRIPT RECENTLY DISCOVERED ALONG THE SOUTH FORELAND HERITAGE COAST, NORTH OF THE WHITE CLIFFS OF DOVER, 83.6 MILES OUTSIDE OF LONDON @ 51.1345*N LATITUDE / 1.3573*E LONGITUDE.

THE DOCUMENT, A LAMBSKIN-BOUND, STITCHED-SPINE BOOK BELIEVED TO BE THE HANDWRITTEN DIARY OF A TEENAGED FEMALE, LIVING IN LONDON, TRAVELING IN DOVER, IN THE LATE NINETEENTH CENTURY, WAS METICULOUSLY RESTORED AND TRANSCRIBED THROUGH A JOINT EFFORT BY GEOLOGISTS AT CAMBRIDGE AND OXFORD UNIVERSITIES, AS MADE POSSIBLE THROUGH A GRANT BY THE BRITISH ROYAL NAVY.

PROF. BARRON FOGGE OVERSAW THE PROJECT UNDER THE DIRECTION OF ADMIRAL ALISTAIR CRONDACK, B.R.N. THE RELIC WAS UNCOVERED BY A YOUNG BOY DIGGING IN THE SAND AT A REMOTE BEACH AT THE AFOREMENTIONED COORDINATES AND TAKEN BY HIS MOTHER TO THE NATURAL HISTORY MUSEUM OF LONDON WHERE CURATORS CONTACTED MILITARY AUTHORITIES.

THE RECLAMATION PROCESS TOOK OVER TWO YEARS TO COMPLETE AND INVOLVED CARBON DATING TO INSURE AUTHENTICITY AND A PAGE BY PAGE RESTORATION TO REMOVE DIRT AND GRIME IMBEDDED INTO THE PARCHMENT PAPER AND A CHEMICAL WASH TO BALANCE DISCOLORATION DUE TO AGE AND EXPOSURE TO WEATHER ELEMENTS.

ALL EFFORTS WERE MADE TO REPRODUCE THE TEXT IN ITS

COMPLETE AND TRUE FORM BUT DUE TO THE LIMITATIONS IN THE RESTORATION PROCESS, SOME INFORMATION HAS BEEN IRRETRIEVABLY LOST. WHEN POSSIBLE THE NOTICE 'DAMAGED BEYOND RESTORATION' WILL APPEAR TO INDICATE A BREAK IN THE TEXT WHERE FURTHER INFORMATION MAY BE MISSING.

THE FOLLOWING DOCUMENT

HAS BEEN CLASSIFIED

TOP SECRET

BY THE BRITISH ROYAL NAVY

ON THE SIXTH DAY OF JULY, IN THE YEAR OF OUR LORD, 1888

~

Mother and I traveled alone following father's announcement he would be unable to accompany us on holiday this summer. I am so very disappointed by father's decision and equally displeased with mother's reaction. "We shall have a good time on our own then," she announced and that was that!

Father's business facilitating the importing and exporting of fine quality handmade rugs and carpets for an eccentric millionaire with the strange moniker Judah Gallows from the region of Tennessee in the far off land across the pacific christened America endeavored to keep father behind his desk, nose to the grindstone, acquiring enough textiles to cover the floors of a sprawling mansion.

So here I sit, mother beside me, father left behind in London, on the second day of our journey, riding the train south to our holiday home as we had each summer solstice, missing terribly the patriarch I so love, while I find my concern for mother's frailty increasing. After a brief illness last winter from which father and I became convinced she would not recover, mother slowly regained her health, and it was decided this trip would aid in her convalescence.

We are scheduled to arrive at the station in Canterbury tomorrow morning at sunrise where arrangements have been made to rendezvous with the horse~drawn coach hired by father to complete the final day of our three day journey to the family's seaside cottage in Dover.

I do long to stand on the veranda at Driftwood Manor ~ the whimsical title father bestowed upon our humble holiday abode ~ and gaze out to sea as the tide breaks against the rocks and the gulls cry out above my head in the cobalt blue of a cloudless July sky. Returning to my White Cliffs each summer is, for me, a return to the true hearth of my heart and I so very much long to reembrace that familiar seaside comfort.

The gentle rocking of the train lulls me toward slumber so I shall retire my writing quill for the night in favor of impending sleep. I look forward to Canterbury at dawn with great anticipation.

ON THE SEVENTH DAY OF JULY, IN THE YEAR OF OUR LORD, 1888 ~

Canterbury was as delightful as I remember, charming me with its hospitality and beauty. We spared time for a hurried brunch ~ kippers with poached eggs and fresh figs ~ before the hour arrived in which we were to set off for Dover. We met the coach at the designated location, introduced ourselves to the driver, and now here I sit, making entries into this journal during the frequent stops necessary in allowing the horses a much needed respite and sip of water as the bouncing of the coach, while in motion, jostles my quill beyond coherent scripture.

We are on schedule to arrive at Driftwood Manor on time, before nightfall and I am anxious as the journey seems to be taking a toll on mother's constitution. She has complained of feeling an unease of stomach and I am afraid she may fall ill on the road, far from the access to a physician's care.

LATER, THE SAME DAY ~

We stopped in Shepherdswell for a tonic. Mother seems to be feeling better. A short delay that may mean we arrive at our destination after dark but worthwhile as it seems to have brought some relief to mother's turbulent tummy. The driver tells us this is the last stop for the horse's replenishment and that he anticipates no further delays.

As I wait to begin the last leg of our journey, my thoughts turn to Robert. When last I saw him, he stood on the platform at the London train station, declaring his intention of making me his wife once I reached the age when it would be appropriate for him to approach my parents seeking permission for the request for my hand in marriage.

I can only confess here in the privacy of this journal that I love him, and I miss him, but his proposition of matrimony frightens me. The man who holds my heart in his hands, the man who aspires to become my husband, has an uncontrolled temper. I fear a life of turmoil and strife should we exchange vows. I have confided in mother my concerns regarding his

****DAMAGED BEYOND RESTORATION****

must be considered should I become Mrs. Robert Charles Vandegault. The driver calls for our departure, I hope to endeavor my quill to confess more, tonight, when I'm comfortably nestled in my bed at Driftwood Manor. More to come.

ON THE EIGHTH DAY OF JULY, IN THE YEAR OF OUR LORD, 1888 ~

Good intentions aside, my quill remained sheaved last evening as I fell straight into slumber the moment I became nestled comfortably in my bed, cocooned in my bedchamber within our family's holiday home. At the end of our three day journey, Driftwood Manor welcomed our tired bodies with the healing amenities of the ocean.

The sea air, the sound of crashing waves, and the distinct cry of the gulls overwhelmed my travel weary senses, casting a hypnotic spell that induced the strangest of dreams. Curious images disconnected to reasoned reality flooded my slumber and chased me into the deepest recesses of the unconscious mind.

When I awoke this morning, I rose refreshed and anxious to explore the cottage beyond the brief candlelight view I had hurriedly observed upon our late night arrival. The White Cliffs call to me but, alas, mother has requested I accompany her to the market this morning as our pantry virtually echoes in its depletion, so my reunion with my beloved White Cliffs will simply have to wait.

LATER, THE SAME DAY ~

Our trek into the local village in Dover expedited the morning and by the time we hauled back the goods mother purchased from the farmer's grocer and the butcher shop, we were tired and weary. Hunger was kept at bay as we stopped along the trail to consume some nuts and dried apples bought at market, but upon our return we fell into a heap near the hearth with exhaustion.

Anticipation abounds! Mother has told me she is inclined to make the short trek with me to take in the view of the White Cliffs should I put off my expedition until sunrise as our trip to the markets of Dover proved taxing enough for her frail state. Feeling the effects of our morning adventure myself, I eagerly agreed. More to come.

ON THE NINETH DAY OF JULY, IN THE YEAR OF OUR LORD, 1888 ~

Mother's malaise seems to have returned, not the serious illness of the prior winter, but a fatigue and nausea similar to the unease she suffered on our coach ride to the coast. She assures me that her discomfort is minor, and I should not worry for her but having seen her so close to death just a few short months ago... well... I simply shan't think of it! Mother's suffering in the cold month of Decem

****DAMAGED BEYOND RESTORATION****

simply no arguing with her. To assure her undisturbed rest, she insists I fulfill our plans for the day and depart on my own from our cottage for an afternoon spent sunning at the White Cliffs. Though I long to return to the shores that I love, I am reluctant to leave mother alone for such an extended time period. What if she should become

****DAMAGED BEYOND RESTORATION****

gathered my paints and brushes into a satchel, folded my easel for carrying, and set out for the day. I shall chronicle my adventures here upon my return.

LATER, THE SAME DAY ~

Dusk falls and what a day I leave behind! With great reluctance I left mother to convalesce in peace and I set off on foot for my magnificent White Cliffs. Following the dirt road that brought horse-drawn coaches through Dover toward the east, I found the narrow pedestrian footpath that rose and fell across the heather covered hills of the Foreland Heritage coastal moors.

Breathing deeply the intoxicating perfume of the wild heather swirling in the salty sea air, while hearing the persistent cries of distant gulls competing to be heard over the sound of crashing waves, as I followed the footpath toward the White Cliffs, overwhelmed my senses.

Struggling with my painting supplies, the walk consumed more time than my remembrances of prior visits, but in little under an hour the view of the horizon dropped off to reveal a shimmering sea far below the cliff's edge, beneath a majestic blue sky and I walked along a high tableau, overlooking the wild sea far below.

As I approached the edge of the White Cliffs, staying safely on the footpath running parallel to the drop-off, more of the sea revealed itself and the wondrous view momentarily stole my breath. How shall I describe the wondrous vista spread out before my awestruck eyes through the insufficient limits of mere language? A grand view such as that presented before me defies simple description and I nearly swooned in appreciation.

After a brief pause to commemorate the moment, I choose to continue along the footpath until the angle of the scenery brought as much inspiration to my paint brush and canvas as it had already bestowed upon my eye. I decided to continue following the path east as it wound its way through the heather strewn moors along the parallel edge of the White Cliffs.

At times, the path curved a little too close to the edge of the White Cliffs for my comfort and I hastened to cling to the opposite side of the path, sometimes even stepping into the wild tangles of foliage outside the path, in my avoidance of the vertigo inducing drop-off.

Father taught me at a very young age of the dangers of the White Cliffs; how the drop-off was a sheer and vertical wall, to always stay on the path, to never wander too close to the unfenced edge. I was seventeen years of age before I was allowed to venture out here on my own and today, as always, I heeded father's warnings and proceeded with the utmost caution.

Suddenly a pair of seagulls dropped out of the sky onto the path before me, startling me into a misstep which resulted into stumbling backward, tripping over my own feet, and landing sorely on my derrière. I sat there, stunned, and watched as the gulls fought over a glistening piece of clam meat clinging to a broken shell.

One squawking bird would snatch it from the other and the other would squawk as it tried to snatch it back. The tug~of~war became vicious as the pair pecked at each other between nips at the clam. The avian mêlée resulted in the shelled morsel rolling over the edge of the abrupt cliff's edge and the pair of gulls diving into flight, chasing after it.

After a moment I stood, brushed the dust and disorientation from my visage, gathered my painting supplies, and continued my way along the footpath. The mid~day sun shone bright in the cobalt sky high above my head, bringing a heated blush to my pallor, and I endeavored to find a shady spot in which to rest.

I rounded the curve in another low~lying, heather~covered hill, and a strange and unexpected sight befell my eyes. A crack in the soil! A break in the ground! A crevasse! A jagged breach in the earth that sliced through the footpath, opening a small canyon that exposed a break in the shear walls of the White Cliffs of Dover like a slice from God's cleaver.

This was a geographical phenomenon that did not exist when last I visited, the prior summer solstice! Perhaps this was the result of an earthquake or some other geological event, which occurred in the interim between visits, but how could such a thing happen without news of it reaching London?

Stepping carefully as I left the footpath, I followed the edge of the crevasse away from the cliff's edge and I pushed my way through the thick foliage in discovery of this new geographic feature. Struggling to make my way through the untamed moors without entangling my painting supplies in the sprawl of the heather's switch, I soon found myself at the wide mouth of the newly emerged canyon.

Having come this far, relatively unscathed, I decided to venture forth. I followed the jagged path into the downward slope of the canyon and all plant life fell away as the terrain became rocky and severe. At times, the angle became so sharp I had to steady myself from falling forward and simply tumbling down the crevasse's slope. In no time at all, the valley in which I traveled closed in and rose up as canyon walls on either side of the increasingly narrow passage.

I became aware of the fact that the sound of the seagull's cry had ceased, the constant hum of the sea breeze was gone, only my heartbeat and the distant sound of waves crashing against rocks rang in my ears. Even the ubiquitous smell of the heather's perfume could not permeate the still air of the canyon, and still I proceeded onward.

At times it seemed as if I were traversing a winding cave, such was the diminishment of sunlight, as I walked ever downward through the crevasse. At other times, the walls closed in so tight, I was required to turn sideways or shimmy in a crouch to force passage, but the idea of turning back never occurred to me. To not explore such a strange and fascinating discovery, to leave unsatisfied such a curiosity, was simply out of the question, so onward I pursued.

Before long, the passage opened, and a magnificent beach front was revealed! The crevasse had cut a passage from the height of the cliff top to the edge of the water! A pristinely white expanse of sparkling sand kept the blue water at bay within a rocky alcove, creating a private beachfront cove, creating a paradise. I stood for a moment, breathless, speechless, looking out to sea. My reaction can only be described as

****DAMAGED BEYOND RESTORATION****

the pristine white sand unblemished save for the tangles of driftwood scattered all about the beach. It was the most spectacular sight my eyes had ever beheld. It was a private paradise, undisturbed by tourist or fishermen. Simply stated, it was the most beautiful place I had ever seen.

At cliff top, I had never ventured close enough to the edge to gaze down the sheer vertical wall of the White Cliffs. Down here at water's edge, gazing straight up the towering expanse, vertigo overcame me, and I returned my gaze down to the shimmering white beachfront spread out before me.

Beautiful and picturesque, the twists of driftwood littered in the multitudes across the sand were like statues sculpted by the sea. Hundreds of branches, tangled and undulating, protruding from the glistening white sand erect or merely lay prone on the expansive beach, the smallest pieces were like little twigs in appearance and the very largest was surely an entire tree trunk, washed ashore from some distant and mysterious forest, grown on the other side of the world.

Once, when I was a mere child of four or five, my father took the entire family on an extended holiday to Fistral Beach, south of Cornwell, and I found a stick of driftwood on the beach and I used it to draw pictures in the sand. When I snapped the stick in half by accident I was sad as there were only a few pieces of driftwood on the beaches of Fistral that day and certainly nothing like the abundantly mass scattering that I found at this seaside utopia where driftwood lay everywhere.

There appeared to be no other people about and I had occasion to wonder if I were the first to discover and explore this strange, new geographical shoreline. I walked up and down the beach, between the snarls of driftwood, convinced of my solitude, for not even the gulls frolicked on this beach, and the overwhelming beauty of the scenery inspired my imagination. Occasionally I heard a strange creaking and crashing sound, like the sound of lightning cleaving a tree trunk into halves, which I attributed to the crashing waves, and the sound of the ocean breaking against the shore.

Unfolding its stand, I mounted my canvas and unsealed my paint jars. The sounds of creaking and moaning continued to ring out yet still it went unnoticed. Taking my easel and brushes from their satchel, I applied bold strokes of blues and blue~greens across the canvass, expressing my interpretation of the sea and sky

****DAMAGED BEYOND RESTORATION****

overcome with hunger as I have completely forgotten about lunch in my awe in this discovery of paradise. Stepping away from my canvas, pleased with my painting's progress, I carried my satchel to the water's edge and consumed the fruit and bread I packed before setting off this morning.

Having never before experienced a single morsel of food at the beach without the annoying persistence of seagulls vying for a portion, I once more found occasion to wonder at their absence. Looking up and down the coastline, I appeared to be the only living creature around for miles, yet...

Looking out to sea, I had a momentary feeling that I was being watched. When I spun around to face the beach, I found only my canvas perched among the scattered driftwood in the secluded cove. I was alone now but for a moment I was sure I was

****DAMAGED BEYOND RESTORATION****

finished with my lunch, I returned to my canvas, retrieved my brush, but I found myself unable to continue. My painting was only half complete, but something was off. I spent several moments comparing my landscape with the scenery all around me and I just couldn't quite put my finger on it.

The only anomaly I could discern between my canvas and its subject I could easily attribute to my inexperience as a painter; my brush's perspective rendered some of my depictions of the driftwood to be further away than they actually appeared in real life, perspective having always been a challenge in which I struggled as a painter.

I shrugged it off at the time and folded away my canvas stand and packed away my brushes and paint jars, but had I taken the time to notice I would have seen that not only were some of the tangled pieces of driftwood closer, they had also changed shape, changed position, and posture, from that which I had painted. That strange crackling sound rang out in the air once more and I shuddered as there was something menacing in its cadence.

Carrying my painting supplies, I ventured my way back through the crevasse, and traversed the footpath along the cliff's edge until I was safely on the road for home. With much anticipation I look forward to tomorrow and my return to this enchanting discovery.

LATER, THE SAME DAY ~

Such joy! Mother seems to be feeling better and is intrigued with my tale of the secret cove. She has declared her desire to accompany me tomorrow should she continue to feel on the upswing, should she feel she could manage the walk. I so hope she can join me! I long to share my discovery! How I should ever find sleep tonight is beyond my hope, excitement abounds.

ON THE TENTH DAY OF JULY, IN THE YEAR OF OUR LORD, 1888 ~

I am so happy to report that mother's health continues to improve but, alas, she has decided she would like to spend some time at the shops in the village and has asked me to accompany her for the day. I so long to return to my beloved White Cliffs and the secret cove of my discovery but I am unable to refuse mother her request so off to town I go. More to come.

LATER, THE SAME DAY ~

After a late start, mother and I set off on our walk to the White Cliffs. Our venture into the town of Dover was abbreviated by striking shopkeepers and after a brief return to our cottage so as to gather my canvass and paint supplies, mother and I found ourselves on the footpath at the opening of the newfound crevasse.

Mother expressed some concern over whether or not she could manage the narrow passage of the canyon, but I assured her that with my help

****DAMAGED BEYOND RESTORATION****

we stepped out of the canyon onto the pristine sands of the hidden and magical beach cove. Mother was as taken aback as I by the breathtaking sight. We shared our delight as we explored the cove together, stepping around and between the various sizes of the scattered driftwood, navigating the private dunes like experienced explorers, as the wind creaked and moaned.

Soon, and not unexpectedly, mother declared herself worn and decided to spread out a quilt so as to lounge for a bit of a nap beneath her parasol. I erected my painting stand in a different position as I had the prior day and mounted a fresh, white canvass to its frame. Keeping mother in view, I decided to include her image in today's rendering of my view of the beach and I set my paint brush to its task.

As the afternoon wore on and an image began to emerge on my canvas, I was once more intrigued by the unusual absence of seagulls or any other wild life at the cove. But as mother slept, and I painted, I was once more overcome with the most uneasy feeling that I was being watched and

****DAMAGED BEYOND RESTORATION****

just as most artists struggle to declare a work finished. Something about this painting had me uneasy but I could not put my finger on what it was that bothered my senses. I briefly debated adding seagulls to my rendering of the sky but decided against the embellishment, for none existed here.

Aware of the strange creaking sound, the agonizing moan was ringing in the air once more. I checked to see that mother was sleeping comfortably beneath her parasol ~ she was ~ and then I washed out my brushes at the water's edge ~ soaking my ankles in the process ~ before returning to my canvas.

I looked at my painting and suddenly I could see it; I could see that which had set my nerves on edge, and I was startled to realize what I had depicted, concerned that I could illustrate such a horror while unaware of the endeavor. Staring at my painting, my mouth fell open and I drew in a sharp breath.

My imagination had created creatures crouching in the sand. Sinewy shapes vaguely rendered through suggestion of form. Branches became limbs. Twigs became tails. Knot holes represented eyes. I had created a menagerie out of the driftwood scattered on the beach and turned them into stalking terrors

A crouching tiger poised to pounce, a coiled snake ready to strike; these figures and more were emerging in my awareness as subtly as the vagueness of their form. But as I looked around this strange, new beach cove I realized that what I was seeing was more than just imagination.

As I looked around me, I could see no movement among the pieces of driftwood scattered about the sand. But I instinctively knew that when I was looking away, when I was studying my canvas, things were creeping in the sand. Some of the driftwood was not driftwood, there were creatures that were using it as camouflage. And they only seemed to move at times when I was not looking.

When I returned my attention to my canvas, I realized that I had drawn a clump of tangled branches as a menacing spider on the far rocks across the beach, but when I looked away from the canvas to the corresponding spot in the sand, the wooden arachnid was much closer, just a few feet away, in fact, from where mother was resting beneath her parasol.

I turned my head toward the canvas, but I kept my eyes slyly focused on the driftwood spider and I involuntarily screamed when I saw it crawl a little closer to mother!

Mother sat up and the driftwood spider immediately ceased its motion, pausing with three legs in the air, mid~step. Mother looked around but she did not see the creature that was stalking her. She admonished me for screaming and inquired as to my state of mind, but I could not bring myself to confess my astounding suspicions regarding the driftwood, preferring a white lie attributing my scream to a misstep and near fall, and I acquiesced to her request to return, post haste, to our cottage.

Tomorrow I shall take you, my journal, my confidant, to my secret cove so as to share my recollections as they occur. I should harbor more fear than I do, but I must know if my imagination has gotten the better of me, played tricks on my logical mind, or if this secret cove is a magical place with mythical creatures. More to come.

ON THE ELEVENTH DAY OF JULY, IN THE YEAR OF OUR LORD, 1888 ~

I have awoken this morning convinced that that which I have come to believe regarding the creatures of driftwood beach to be nothing more than my over active imagination. Days of exhausting travel, worry over mother's health, my melancholy over father's absence, all combined to wear on my nerves, and it is understandable to my reason that my weary eyes or tired mind should play tricks on me.

Still, I arose from my bed with a sense of excitement and anticipation, and I vacated my bedchamber well before dawn to prepare for my return to the secret cove. Having gathered my painting supplies and a satchel of food for the day, I needed merely to wait until sunrise to bid farewell to mother ~ who declared her intention to rest for the day ~ before I set off on the footpath toward the White Cliffs.

Shortly, as I walked among the heather-covered hills of the

coastal moors, I had come to convince myself that the strange new crevasse that had suddenly breached the cliff-side would have disappeared just as mysteriously as it had appeared, as a figment of my imagination. But as I crested the next hill, the haunting canyon came into view.

Traversing the rocky terrain, I navigated my way down to the magical beach cove strewn with driftwood (or ?) and I wasted no time in erecting my painting stand and mounting a fresh, blank canvass. At first I struggled to bring a brushstroke to the white void of the canvass as I found myself unable to interpret what I was seeing. Despite the lack of seagulls and the persistence of that strange creaking sound, all appeared normal.

The beachfront seemed as nothing more than a beachfront, the driftwood seemed as nothing more than driftwood, and I seemingly appeared nothing more than a fool. Surely my imagination had run rampant on prior visits. Perhaps I had suffered from hallucination-inducing sunstroke.

Feeling clear of head and light in heart, convinced my foolishness regarding the driftwood was simply that, I took my brush to the canvass with a flourish of inspiration. Never have I rendered a complete landscape as confidently and swiftly and soon I was looking at

****DAMAGED BEYOND RESTORATION****

My stomach grumbled as I washed out my paint brushes at the water's edge and after poking them in the sand, bristles up, to dry, I found a shady spot on the rocks near the cliff slope, and I ate my lunch while watching the waves crash against the surf.

Sated, sleepy, I spread out the quilt mother insisted I bring, and I lay for a quick nap. It was not an unconscious decision to pick a spot that was relatively devoid of nearby driftwood, the closest significant piece being at least ten meters away, as precaution prevails over rampant imagination, and I drifted to sleep watching the smaller, twisted little twigs scattered closer by which I assumed, based on their size, to be harmless, while listening to that strange creaking sound crackling in the salty air.

But when I awoke, a short time later, the quilt was covered with dozens of those little driftwood twigs, and I was covered in small, bite-like welts on the exposed areas of my arms, legs, and face. I screamed and sat up, shaking little pieces of driftwood from me. I stood up, grabbing the quilt as I rose, and I shook it to remove the driftwood clinging on.

It was then that I noticed a rather large piece of driftwood, tangled into the shape of a giant crab, which had not been there when I lay for my nap, had crawled within two meters from where my head had lain. Two twisted branches, sprouting from the sides of the wooden beast, into the shape of claws, were frozen in the pose of reaching out toward the spot where I had slept.

But again, nothing moved as I watched, tempting doubt. Yet there could be no doubting the pain of the dozens of little wounds on my exposed flesh, and the redness of their abrasions, some of which were starting to bleed.

Shaking, I made a mad dash to my canvas, resolved to pack up and leave the cove, never to return, when I was stopped in my tracks by what I discovered within my painted landscape. I stood there before it with my mouth hung open in disbelief.

The driftwood creatures were all around me, closing in on me, stalking me! Once again I had painted a menagerie of twisted, wooden creatures, crouching in the sand, surrounding me as I painted, unaware! The driftwood tiger was there, just a few feet to my right, hunched back into position to spring up and pounce! The driftwood snake was nearby, coiled and venomous, and the driftwood spider

****DAMAGED BEYOND RESTORATION****

There is more than just one spider among the shapes of driftwood!

I ran, leaving my canvas and satchel of painting supplies behind, and I nearly stumbled as I scrambled toward the opening of the crevasse and my escape from this cursed beach. But as I approached the path that led back up to the moors and the way home, the ground shook and all was

****DAMAGED BEYOND RESTORATION****

a devastating earthquake resulting in a landslide. A cascade of falling rocks that cut off the path out of the hidden cove. A cave-in of the canyon and I am trapped as a cluster of driftwood spiders crawl

****DAMAGED BEYOND RESTORATION****

must realize that I am trapped as they have dropped all pretense of stealth and now move freely in my view. It was also in that moment that I realized that the strange crackling, moaning sound that I had previously attributed to the salty sea wind was, in actuality, the creak and groan of the driftwood creature's limbs and muscles contracting and expanding as they crept through the sand. They move much slower than the creatures they represent but I am out-numbered, trapped, and

****DAMAGED BEYOND RESTORATION****

have been able to outrun the army of driftwood spiders but I was cornered at the water's edge by a pack of driftwood tigers. In a low crouch, they moved with feline stealth and menace.

Ambushed, I stumbled, and for a moment, with that advantage, the closest driftwood tiger took a swipe at me with its wooden paw, and it tore a row of slashes down my top-skirt, bloodying my leg from knee to ankle.

Smelling blood, the other driftwood tigers clamored.

I was able to escape further damage from their wooden claws by swimming a little ways out into the surf where the driftwood tigers seemed reluctant to follow and I swam ashore a short distance up the sand only to come out of the water to encounter a cluster of driftwood scorpions. The gnarled beasts approached with barbed branch stingers poised to attack.

****DAMAGED BEYOND RESTORATION****

found refuge in a small alcove, cut into the base of the cliff-side. It is here that I have been able to document the astounding event of my final visit to this mysterious beach in this faithfully inscribed journal I can only pray that it does not prove to stand as my final testament.

A cluster of driftwood spiders are cresting the mound of rocks at the water's edge, and the wooden snakes slither closer to the entrance of the shallow cave in which I hide! The driftwood tigers sniff the air for scented clues as to my whereabouts and turn their gnarled necks toward my hiding place! I see what appears to be a dragonfly, and another mass in the shape of a bat! I pray these creatures lack the aerodynamics to fly! I have come to see that the largest of these beasts, that which was surely an entire tree trunk, lying on its side, was in the form of a huge centipede, its torso lined with angled branches that crawled in the sand like rows of insect~like legs! Huge wooden pinchers snap in the air as it slowly approaches! I will hide this diary in the sand, thankful to have one last chance to declare my love to my mother and father as I fear that all shall be

****DAMAGED BEYOND RESTORATION****

EDITOR'S NOTE

AS A MATTER OF HISTORICAL RECORD, THE BODY OF VICTORIA ELIZABETH COLLINGSWORTH – BELIEVED TO BE THE AUTHOR OF THE PRECEDING DOCUMENT – WAS NEVER FOUND FOLLOWING THE REPORT OF HER DISAPPEARANCE BY HER MOTHER, MARY COLLINGSWORTH, ACCORDING TO CONSTABLE RECORDS DISCOVERED IN THE DOVER TOWN HALL ARCHIVES.

MR. ROBERT CHARLES VANDEGAULT, WHO WAS RUMORED AT THE TIME TO BE MISS COLLINGSWORTH'S FIANCÉ, WAS HELD FOR QUESTIONING BY SCOTLAND YARD DETECTIVES, CALLED IN TO OVERSEE THE MISSING PERSON'S INVESTIGATION. NO ARRESTS WERE EVER MADE.

SCOTLAND YARD CLOSED THE CASE WITH AN 'UNRESOLVED' STATUS ON NOVEMBER 5, 1888.

THE PRECEDING DOCUMENT WAS DISCOVERED LAST YEAR AFTER A RARE 6.8 MAGNITUDE EARTHQUAKE OPENED A DEEP CREVASSE IN THE SHORELINE NEAR THE VILLAGE OF DOVER, KENT, REVEALING A PREVIOUSLY UNKNOWN BEACHFRONT.

TODAY, UNDER PROTEST FROM THE RESTORATION TEAMS AT CAMBRIDGE AND OXFORD, THE BRITISH ROYAL NAVY HAS CONFISCATED ALL MATERIALS AND DOCUMENTS RELATING TO THE JOURNAL AND HAS SHUT OUT THE PROFESSORS WHO ARE LOOKING FOR FURTHER ANSWERS REGARDING THE DISAPPEARANCE OF RESTORATON TEAM LEADER, PROF. BARRON FOGGE.

MOST ALARMINGLY, VERIFIED REPORTS HAVE CONFIRMED THAT THE BRITISH ROYAL NAVY HAS QUARANTINED A THREE

MILE SECTION OF THE SOUTH FORELAND HERITAGE COASTLINE NEAR THE WHITE CLIFFS OF DOVER AND A SCIENTIFIC TEAM SPECIALIZING IN THE WEAPONIZATION OF ORGANIC LIFE FORMS FOR USE IN MILITARY OPERATIONS HAS BEEN SPOTTED SETTING UP A LABORATORY IN THE AREA.

WHEN ASKED FOR COMMENT, ADMIRAL ALISTAIR CRONDACK AND VARIOUS REPRESENTATIVES OF THE BRITISH ROYAL NAVY REMAIN SILENT.

THE PRECEDING DOCUMENT

HAS BEEN CLASSIFIED

TOP SECRET

BY THE BRITISH ROYAL NAVY

CASE FILE:

CLOSED

******END OF DOCUMENT******

STORY COPYRIGHTS

MIRROR IMAGE
CAT & MOUSE
THE CREATURES OF DRIFTWOOD BEACH

KILL IT!
THE NAG
UNDER THE BED

FACE LIFT
TWO HEADS ARE BETTER THAN ONE
BOO!
SECRET SANTA

Made in the USA
Columbia, SC
23 November 2021

49635417R00089